Hannah

Hannah

A novel by Ruthanne Nopson

ReadersMagnet, LLC

This book is dedicated to orphans everywhere.

*And in memory of Uncle Frank,
friend to every child.*

Hannah
Copyright © 2023 by Ruthanne Nopson

Published in the United States of America
ISBN   Paperback: 978-1-960629-07-4
ISBN   Hardback: 978-1-960629-44-9
ISBN   eBook: 978-1-960629-08-1

All rights reserved. No part of this publication may be reproduced, stored in a retrieval system or transmitted in any way by any means, electronic, mechanical, photocopy, recording or otherwise without the prior permission of the author except as provided by USA copyright law.

The opinions expressed by the author are not necessarily those of ReadersMagnet, LLC.

ReadersMagnet, LLC
10620 Treena Street, Suite 230 | San Diego, California, 92131 USA
1.619. 354. 2643 | www.readersmagnet.com

Book design copyright © 2023 by ReadersMagnet, LLC. All rights reserved.

Cover design by Kent Gabutin
Interior design by Dorothy Lee

TABLE OF CONTENTS

CHAPTER 1	Hannah	9
CHAPTER 2	Sam Sam	23
CHAPTER 3	The Visitors	30
CHAPTER 4	The Decisions	42
CHAPTER 5	The Midnight Train	47
CHAPTER 6	Meeting David	64
CHAPTER 7	Driving Danny Boy	72
CHAPTER 8	Jiggidy Jig	83
CHAPTER 9	Getting Ready For The Christmas Party	95
CHAPTER 10	The Christmas Party	107
CHAPTER 11	The Engagement	117
CHAPTER 12	To Grandfather R's House, We Go	122
CHAPTER 13	The New Year	131
CHAPTER 14	Wedding Plans	138
CHAPTER 15	The Village	150
CHAPTER 16	Off To College	154
CHAPTER 17	Those Love Ly Weekends	160
CHAPTER 18	The Wedding Of David And Hannah	163

HANNAH

CHAPTER 1

Europe gave up generations of children, artists, writers, industrialists, and their finest minds in the nineteenth century. For decades, The immigrants came by ship to the new continent of America. Men of steel, renown, and wealth crowed onto vessels filled with the humble, weak, and brokenhearted, longing for the blessings of Liberty. But the angry sea had no favorites, charm, or repose, and all succumbed to the same icy fingers that brought the victims down to the hostile chambers of death in the Atlantic Ocean.

Among the poor was the Zimmer family from Wurttembergers, Germany, in the late summer of 1900. Jacob, a slight man about five foot four, with piercing eyes that make you listen to him, has dark brown thick hair and a full mustache, was high on dreams and low on money. Mable, his devoted wife, was frail but intense in spirit and devotion to her husband and children, Hannah, age eleven, and -Lilly, age eight. Hannah was not happy she was leaving the motherland. Their family life would change in language, customs, and food, but they are ready to support their Papa and help their Mama. Hannah felt uncertain and full of doubt about the future. Maybe this is a warning from God. In her heart, something was not going to turn out the way Papa planned. She pondered these things in the rough, sleepless nights on SS Alemania moving towards The New York Harbor. The grateful and tired passengers were anxious to leave their prison-like confinement. The last few weeks were full of discomfort, unsanitary conditions, people vomiting, and wrenching in pain.

After many days and weeks at sea, the Zimmer family of four stayed huddled together on the ship's stern. After days of seeing nothing but the cold Atlantic Ocean, they felt like nameless shadows. Was Papa's dream coming true? He wanted to enter the New York Harbor in daylight, and so it was.

The early morning light blanketed the New York City skyline with low clouds and fog. The cold rain and trembling waves didn't keep the smile off Jacob Zimmer's face.

"Look kinder," look at the golden sun peeking through clouds stretching 0ver New York City. "There she is, "Lady Liberty welcomed us to her land of the free and home of the brave. Kinder," see how she stands tall with her torch held high and the book in her hand? Our names are in the book. Soon we will be part of The Promised Land. She is a grand lady that will light our way to a new life. We must give all we have to this blessed country; Lady Liberty will give back our dreams."

The SS Alemannia Captain guided his ship into New York Harbor at Ellis Island. The immigrants received paperwork to become American citizens and begin their new life. English was the first thing to learn. Hannah felt confident in learning English and knew words like hello, goodbye, please, and thank you. Papa knew a few words that he said were English. Mama is unsure about learning a new language. She will depend on the girls and Jacob to speak English. Lilly thought English sounded like a bunch of muttering. Lilly knew Hannah would be there for her. Hannah was always there.

The family had to learn English and American customs, find a place to live, and find a job for Papa.

They moved into a dreary, dark tenement building near Orchard Street in New York City. "German Town' was not far away. They wanted to settle close to the seventeenth ward, where many families from Wurttemberg had established their new homes. Jacob hoped his family would meet other German-speaking families. They had to move into the second floor of a tenement building. Jacob worried it would be hard for Mama to adjust to their new home. Hannah thought a dog or cat would be dumb to live in a place like New York City. The family didn't have many personal possessions, so it didn't"t take long to put away the dishes and make up the beds in the two-bedroom apartment. Mama was sensitive to her children's needs. She knew Hannah was struggling to adjust to their new life. Lilly happily curled up next to Mama, listening to a scary fairy tale story or planning tea parties for her dolls.

One day Mama had an idea. She called the girls together. "I know all of us are lonesome for Germany. It would be fun to do the same things here as in the old country."

"Like what?" said Hannah "We could go on a picnic. Bake cookies, or we could have a sing-along."

"Nothing here reminds me of Germany or our farm," complained Hannah.

That evening She went outside and sat on the rough cement steps and drab surroundings. After dinner on the farm, the families gathered at the Zimmer farmhouse. The men talked about farms and raising a garden, while the women spoke about children and baking. They would tell stories of the olden days. Sometimes the children thought the stories were fairy tales. They didn't care; this was the best of times. The family was together, the young and the old. In the morning, the women would gather together in the village kitchens. They would bring bread dough and let it rise in the warming ovens. While waiting for the soft, sticky substance to rise and bake, the woman would sew or knit and catch up on the latest gossip. Small children ran around the kitchen or played outside. The men went to the nearby pool room or tavern. The aroma of freshly baked bread filled the air. There would be different ovens in a few decades; people would recognize an unusual smell With a sigh, Hannah chose to try being happy. She looked at the wooden sidewalks. She remembered grassy meadows the children ran through, taking them on new adventures, smelling the fresh air, playing in the greenest pastures by the still waters, and making necklaces out of sweet clover. Crystalline, cold and pure, sparkling streams contently found their way to the nearest river or lake. It was fun to skip rocks on the streams; sometimes, the children would jump in for a swim in summer's warmth. Trees dressed in their most beautiful apparel showed off their pink blossoms while shading regiments of flowers that loved the cool shade. She longed for a taste of the cold water from the creeks.

Foul-smelling water ran in ditches down the street in front of the tenement building. The pleasure of skipping rocks in a stream or climbing a tree is gone. Now Hannah can't climb a leafy tree on a summer day. She had to climb cement stairs, and you can't skip rocks in a wash basin. Buildings tall and gray took the place of the oak tree she loved to climb. Papa made a treehouse for all of the children. The sounds of the city were busy, people hurrying one way and people rushing the other way. She might hear a bird singing his little song if she had listened long enough, but she couldn't see him. She felt sorry for the horses pulling their heavy burdens down the dusty streets. It must be hard for horses to live in the city. "I am sure they would like to get away from here and lay down in the tender grass of their home," thought Hannah. She laughed, imagining being rescued by a white horse carrying a handsome prince and riding into the colorful sunset, melting into delicate pink and lavender, splashed with the palest red and brilliant gold. That only happens in fairy tales. She thought the sun rose and set in a different direction now that she was across the Atlantic. She would find out from Papa. On her way back up the cold stairs to her family, she saw a broom leaning against a door in the hallway. She shuttered at its sight. Her boy cousins told her stories about witches, and if she ever saw a broom, it probably belonged to a witch who chases little girls, and they were never heard from again. She ran upstairs and couldn't wait to get into her home.

 Tears dripped down Hannah's cheeks, remembering the good times that once were and will never be.

 November brought gray skies too strong to allow the weak sun to make its brief morning appearance. Icy raindrops pelted the grimy windowpanes, leaving little rivers of tears as if it was running down a young girl's cheeks.

Papa's pocket watch was resting on the nightstand, reminding Hannah and Lilly it was time to get up, get ready for school, and take care of Mama, who was very sick. The girls could hear Papa in the kitchen stoking the wood and coal fire on the stove and the happy tea kettle bubbling. It's t" time for tea Hannah tugged on Lilly's brownish-red curls and said: "Time to get up, little sister, silly little Lilly, silly little Lilly May."

"I don't want to get up. IT'S cold in here," complained Lilly "Leiden," get up; you need to take care of Mama and get ready for school. Papa poked his head in the bedroom door and smiled at his two daughters.

"We are getting up, papa," yawned Hannah. We will take care of Mama now. It is hard for the girls to see their Mama so sick. She was the healthy one that took care of everybody. The doctor thinks she has typhoid fever. Many people in the neighborhood and their buildings are sick with the same thing. It may have started on the ship. The doctor told the family to boil water for twenty minutes before washing dishes or cooking potatoes and tea. Many patients vomit, get dehydrated, and have a high fever. Papa hugged the girls and went out the door to his long workday at the livery stable. Jacob knew how to clean up after horses. The money he earned and saved was for his bakery. He hoped he brought enough from Germany to pay the rent and buy food.

"Lilly, do you want me to walk you outside to the toilet? "I know you don't like to go there alone."

"No!" I'm going to use Mama's chamber jar. But I do not want to go out in the rain!"

"May I remind you, silly little Lilly, we are not to use the chamber jar unless it is an emergency?'

"Banana toes, this is an emergency!"

"I will make Mama some tea and soft, boiled eggs. Then, you brush her hair, help her get dressed, put face cream on her hands and feet, another thing", ordered Hannah. I do this every day, interrupted Lilly, don't be so bossy, and go back into the ketch."Lilly got a towel, hairbrush, and skin cream ready to take to Mama.

Hannah was ready to dish up soft-boiled eggs and bread when she heard Lilly. Screaming, she wiped her hands on her apron and rushed into Mama's bedroom.

"Are you ok? Are you hurt?" asked Hannah "Hannah, I think Mama is dead, cried Lilly. Look at her; she is not moving The girls looked at the lifeless form buried under heavy quilts.
They could not touch her.

The sisters held each other and cried. "What are we going to do without, mama?" cried Lilly.

"Now we have to look after Papa, and he will have to look after us," said Hannah

Both girls ran through the kitchen and down the dim hallway. Together they knocked on Frau Bruno's door. Slowly the door opened, revealing a tall, smiling lady. Her dark hair is tied to her head like a doorknob. More than ample bosoms rested like soft pillows on her thick waist. Her breasts moved like biscuits on the stew when she leaned over to speak to the children.

"Gout morgen kinder, vote are you doing here so early, before school?"

"It's our mama," sobbed the girls. Something is wrong; she won't move or say anything. She might be dead."

"Come in, mien liber, sit at the table with my sons, you know them. Gus, Charles, and Henry. The boys smiled shyly at the two girls. Sit down and have some bread and jam."

"Don't worry about a thing; I will take care of it for you. I am going now to check on your Mama. Then I will find your Papa. Hurry off to school; you can stay here until he comes home. I will tell him you will be here."

Frau Bruno searched for two hours to find Papa. Finally, she saw him coming out of a livery stable and told him his beloved wife, Mable, had passed away. Jacob nearly fainted and could not keep tears from flowing down his cheeks. Frau Bruno invited the family for supper.

She told Papa there was a German Lutheran Church not far away, and she would go with him tomorrow to plan funeral services. Frau Bruno also reminded Papa he should go to church more often. She would be happy to take the children.

About nine o'clock the following day, Frau Bruno knocked on Zimmer's door. Lilly opened the door to a smiling lady who said, "Guten Morgan," are you ready to go to the church?"

"Come in," said Papa. "We are ready."

The crispiness of autumn escorted the four mourners to their destination.

"There is the church on the left. Can you see the steeple?" Frau Bruno, almost out of breath.

Shadows-like silhouettes of four souls rippled up the long narrow stairs of the church. Papa opened the door for the ladies and entered the narthex. The familiar odors of waxed floors and a small oil stove reminded them of their church in Germany.

They approached the sanctuary and saw tapers resting on the altar—the flickering candles inviting them to the House of God. Stained glass windows designed with figures of the Good Shephard and His flocks are watching over the congregation. When church members come to worship their Lord, chairs in straight rows wait for the worshipers, and the organ is anxious to play familiar hymns. Hannah felt a sense of relief when she looked at a message board written in German.

The little group heard the sound of heavy footsteps coming toward them.

"Guten Aubin," said the medium-tall pastor with silver hair and dressed in clerical clothing, coming toward them. He extended his hand to Jacob and said, "welcome." Are you here for the graveside service for Nrs Zmmwe? I am Pastor Dengler," and you must be Frau Bruno?" "

"I am sorry for your loss," said the kind pastor shaking his hand Jacob.

"Hannah and Lilly are my little frau lines."

"Hello," said Hannah in a low voice. Standing close to her, Lilly said' "hello, pastor."

We have no money for a service, said Jacob trying to hold back his tears. But, we can stand by the grave, pray, and sing songs."

Overwhelmed with fear, sadness, and disbelief, the four souls huddled together and walked arm linked to arm to the church graveyard, the garden of the voiceless. Hannah rested her head on Papa's shoulder, clinging to his arm. She could smell his old woolen coat, which he had worn all her life. It reminded her of a life that evaporated into them somewhere across the sea.

Lilly rested her head on Papa's scratchy coat sleeve. Streams of tears ran down her cheeks like raindrops on a windowpane.

The earth yielded dark, dank, lifeless clay, defending the ossuary where Mama would rest in eternity. The fragile, motionless form of Mabel Lillian Zimmer lay swaddled in satin covers and pillows, a tiny woman without life. They would behold her no more. The preacher said Mama's spirit returned to heaven, and God gave it. How Can this be.? T Hannah had no idea. She gazed at her blessed mother, yet she was supposed to be in heaven with God. She was here. How did her spirit get to the far-above heavenly places? Hannah could not understand. Her heart was too frail and broken to learn the ways of grown-ups. And how would she explain this to Lilly? How would Papa tell it?

The only thing she could understand was that she and Lilly were motherless. She would have to take care of Lilly. Papa needed her too.

Who would take care of her and give her strength, love, AND wisdom? She looked to the heavens, hoping the answers would be there. The preacher man said God was up there; maybe He was looking down at her.

After the brief graveside service, the mourners walked arm in arm toward a useless sunset. Their shadows stretched like new arrows, ready to fly past the moon and the stars.

Motionless and weary, the Zimmer family climbed the stairs to their tenement building. Hannah decided to sit outside and collect her thoughts. She could hear Frau Bruno calling the Zimmer family to come in for supper. She prepared a tasty chicken stew, biscuits, and red jam.

The emotions of the day made Hannah tired and exhausted. The evil city became a skyline of ghostly dragons and demons ready to capture her soul. Gargoyle faces and s hideous sounds, and various odors blast her face. Raw sewage running down the streets turned into a green slim, ready to gobble her alive.

Sheets hanging on the clotheslines between the buildings looked like ghosts flying in the night wind, jeering and laughing at her. Hannah felt like she was in hell! The cold concrete stair step received the young maiden swoon and tears like raindrops washing away daily grime. Hidden deep inside, she could barely remember "mama." Why did you leave? Why is heaven so far away? How can I teach Lilly and Henry to pronounce their words, Papa can't cook, but he can bake. Lilly would rather play with dolls than study. She calls me Hannah's banana nose. Please show me the heavenly places. Hannah felt something touching her. It was Frau Bruno. A soft voice sounded like an angel saying to Hannah, "I will come to your home, read to you and stay by your bedside until you and Lilly fall asleep." whispers Frau Bruno.

With tears in her eyes and a grateful heart, Hannah and Frau Bruno climbed the steps to an evening of rest and safety. Hannah remembered a Bible verse that said God is always with us and will never leave us. Was Frau Bruno the hand of God?

The Zimmer family became a song without a melody, a candle without a flicker, and a diamond without luster. The wisdom and beauty of Mama are gone. Yet, Jacob could often capture a glimpse of his beloved in his two daughters; a distinct voice or look, a burst of laughter, made him feel that Mama was near.

Life became difficult for Jacob Zimmer. His desire for a new life without his beloved Mable seemed impossible. He didn't take as much interest in his children as he should. He knew nothing about raising little girls; how could he explain they're coming into young womanhood? How could he choose their clothes or put their hair in a curl? But it would have to happen soon. Tomorrow he would talk to Frau Bruno.

Autumn is harvest season and rewards for reaping the spoils of the farmer's fields. The sun would not linger as long, and the

HANNAH

Night patterns covered all landscape for a winter's rest. Jacob knew he was in the autumn of his life, and the harvest he reaped had to be successful; his yield was Hannah and Lilly. Hannah suspected Papa was up to something that would not bring good news. He offered the children a picnic in the park and candy and maybe ice cream. That had never happened. They had no money to expect luxuries like that. He has been talking to Frau Bruno a lot. They spoke in whispers when the girls were near. So what is going on? Hannah thought she would be cagy and be ready for the bad news. Papa told his girls he was taking them to a new home, and they would go there in the morning. Today they will pack their meager belongings. They will go tomorrow, which is Saturday Hannah and Lilly worried all night about where they were going to live. Hannah stressed that a witch might live there.

The Zimmer family got up early the following day, and the girls packed their possessions.

"I will carry a bag for each of you. If you get tired, we will rest in the park and eat the sandwiches you girls made. Think of this as a fun adventure," advised Jacob Zimmer.

Hannah and Lilly didn't have much to say. All they knew was they would sleep in a different place tonight.

"How much further do we have to go?" grumbled Lilly.

"Not far, said papa. See that church steeple ahead of us in the distance? That's where we are going. Can you hear the church bells ringing?"

"Are we going to live at a church?" asked Lilly. "No, Hannah; it's one of the places for orphans."

Hannah could only feel anger in her heart towards her father. Frau Bruno helped him choose this place.

"That means it is a home for children who have no parents. "Now, my children, it is not that bad. The home is expecting us today. They will welcome you."

"See the large Building A. That is where you will stay. Building B is for the boys. Look at the large playground. You will be comfortable here and have a lot more room."

Jacob Zimmer hugged and kissed his fraud lines. He assured them he would be back for a visit.

The trio climbed the suitable stairs to Building A and rang the doorbell. A smiling Sister answered the door.

"Welcome and come in. Are you the Zimmer family? We have been expecting you."

"Set your bundles down, and I will go and get Wister Catherine. You may call me Sister Lois."

"This place is a Catholic Church and orphanage, not Lutheran like we are," snapped Hannah.

The front hall is full of children of all ages. Some were sitting at a table doing homework. Some of the children are noisy toddlers throwing toys and chasing each other.

Hannah and Lilly looked out the window of the front hall. They saw papa blowing kisses and waving to them. Hannah is sure he won't be back for visits. He is free now. He could even go back to Germany.

The First Night in the Catholic Orphanage was lonely and frightening, especially for Lilly. Her world had collapsed. She must have roommates because there are two empty beds. Nothing was familiar in that big scary room where she would sleep and live. The worse thing was that Hannah was in a different room; she didn't know where. : Lilly had never been without her Sister. And I would never trust grown-ups again, not even Frau Bruno.

Hannah worried about Lilly. She must be so frightened to be in a strange place alone. They went on many adventures around the city after Mama passed away, but the girls were never separated. Hannah remembered the fun of meeting with other children who had no parents or one parent and were running around New York City. They used the same tactics to find their way home to the motherland. The children stayed in groups looking after one another when they would go into the woodlands. They climbed a tree or marked a path; they always found a home. Now there was nothing, no pathway; there was nothing familiar. Hannah felt like she was on misery row, and she did not know if she would l be able to forgive Papa and Frau Bruno. The orphanage was full of adults and children; she didn't know them. There was very little privacy or attention, no bedtime stories or stories of the old country. Understanding the minds of grown-ups is still a mystery. When she grows up, she will not keep secrets from her children or suddenly put them in a new place without notice. They left Germany with just themselves to start a new life. How could she and Lilly be happy without grandparents, aunts, uncles, and cousins? All she has is Lilly, and she will find a way to share a room with her precious little sister once again. Hannah fell asleep, feeling sure of her plans to run away.

The shank of midnight spread her fabulous cape over the New York City skyline. The city slumbered while waiting for dawn to make her entrance with the morning sun. Hannah and Lilly had been at the orphanage for almost three months, and papa, and Frau Bruno, had not come to visit them; they knew the rules of discipline. One midnight Hannah stood on her tiptoes in the cold darkness, resting her elbows on the cold window sill, and looked through the dirty pane of glass at the city that haunted her. Even the moon, in her fullness, cast mysterious shadows through the window and across the hall. All Hannah could think about was Mama passing away and their Papa giving them away. Today is not the new life she expected. Maybe someday, the Sisters would understand what it is like to be separated from their Sister and not live together as sisters.

While Hannah was daydreaming about what her life should be like, she heard swishing robes, hollow footsteps approaching, and paraphernalia thumping back and forth from a Sister's circumference, clanking like they were plotting against her.

The sound came closer, and Hannah heard her name, "Hannah Rose!" what are you doing in the hallway? It's past your bedtime." Hannah slowly turned her head and saw something with the man's face on the moon, circled with a white halo, gliding toward her. A voice of authority said, "Go to bed like a good girl, and I will see you at morning prayers."

Hannah laughed to herself as the dark form melted into the darkness. If those Sisters had any idea how much she hated it and how she would find a way to escape the old Sisters who fly around on their brooms. Hannah had to have a secret plan to look for Papa and Frau Bruno and maybe return to Germany.

Gloomy and weary was the following day, much like Hannah herself. But melodies from the unseen birds did lift her spirit. She thought if a bit of bird could sing on a gray morning, she should quit feeling sorry. Today is the day she and Lilly will form a secret escape plan. She will find Lilly and tell her about leaving this awful place forever! They would go to Papa and live happily ever after, just like in the storybooks.

Lilly was busy playing games in the schoolyard with other children. Then, she saw Hannah and ran toward her saying, "I have a big secret to tell you!" Lilly loved secrets and quickly ran to her Sister. She, too, had some information that nobody else knew. Or at least something to share.

Hannah told Lilly," you tell your news first. Then I will tell you mine".

Hannah put her arm around Lilly's small shoulder and said, "Silly Lilly, what is your big secret?"

Lilly said, "This secret is about the trains we hear at night. They are those big black things that make a lot of noise and puff smoke. When people get on those things, you never see them again. Remember Tanta Emma? Papa took her to the train, and we never saw her again."

"If we ride on a train from here, that will happen to us. The sisters put the children on a train, and no one ever sees them again. That could happen to us".

Hannah said, "at least we would get away from here."

"I have some better news that you will like. We will sneak out of here and find Papa and maybe Frau Bruno. They have not visited us since we have been here."

"Maybe," said Lilly, they had to get on a train and can't get back here."

Hannah was ready to explain to Lilly her plan to escape; when interrupted by a sweet-sounding voice.

"I need to talk to both of you now!"

Sister Catherine caught up with Hannah and Lilly, took their hands, and hurried into the front hall and the office of Sister Agnus.

"Sister Catherine, please bring in the new roommate for the Zimmer girls," said Sister Agnus in her tired at the end of the day voice

Sister Catherine left the room. When she returned said, "Hannah and Lilly, meet Samuel, your new roommate!"

Sister Agnes was sitting behind her desk, looking small and frail, shuffling papers and making notes. She stopped, folded her hands in prayer, and looked up at the children.

"I have some more news for the two of you." said the Sister. "I know you would like to share the same bedroom so I will arrange it. However, there will be another roommate.

The girls looked at each other and said they like to make new friends, especially if they can be together.

Lilly pointed her finger. And said do you mean him? He is a boy."

"We know he is a little boy! Snapped Sister Agnes; that's why he is your new roommate."

The pint-sized boy said his name was Samuel. He has dark brown hair, a few ringlets resting on his forehead, and a big smile. We found him on the front porch with the name Samuel pinned to his worn coat. That is the only thing we know about him". Said Sister Agnus

"Sister Catherine and I want to move you and Lilly to a larger room. There is a double bed in there. I will have a crib brought in. for now. We will find a single bed somewhere, said Sister Agnus. You will take care of Samuel?."

With love running through her heart, Hannah went over to Samuel, knelt before him, took his little hands in hers, and said, "Samuel, your coat is tattered and worn. The sleeves are too short, and you only have one button. I will make you a new coat."

Hannah made him a little coat and brought it to him yearly.!
Samuel 2-19

SAM SAM

CHAPTER 2

Hannah felt it was time to rest before the evening meal. She had worked in the vegetable garden and pulled weeds. Winter is on its way. She has to help keep the plants healthy for winter meals in the orphanage. She helped with endless laundry. It is hard work to help lift large pots of water. Heat the water, scrub the clothes, rinse and hang the clothes on the clothesline to dry.

If a girl wanted her dress ironed, she had to do it herself. There were several irons of various sizes heating' on the wood stove.

Hannah and Lilly had watched Mama and Grandmother Zimmer do laundry and iron, but they had never tried it. The girls never thought of doing that hard work, especially at a young age.

Some of the girls had burn marks on their dresses or skirt in the shape of an iron. Hannah hoped Lilly would be better at ironing. Hannah would instead work in the garden. Lilly signed up for hand sewing and embroidery lessons. She wanted to work in the kitchen and learn baking bread and cookies like her grandmother and grandfather Zimmer.

While Hannah lay in bed, she always noticed the ceiling with various water sports and hanging strips of ceiling paper. She was on the third floor and thought there was a roof above her room. Hannah and Lilly would try to solve the mystery. Hannah also noticed a wall hanging with a man hanging on a cross. One of the Sisters told her the image was a crucifix, and the man on the cross was Jesus. How could that be? She thought. As a child, Hannah and Lilly learned Jesus was in heaven. So, where is He now? Hanna noticed many cobwebs in the corners, curtains, and windows. They looked like harry little goblins that would tease her in the Night. The room had no mirrors or pictures.

Hannah stretched and yawned. The supper would be ready soon. She thought she heard raindrops on the window near her. She looked through the dirty pane of glass—drops of rain flowing down the window like tears on a young girl's cheers. Hannah looked out the window at the New York City skyline. The city has no hopes, futures, or dreams. Green slime was running down the street in ditches; just like her sadness, she remembered Mama's death a year ago. She placed a tiny, frail woman swaddled in satin lying in a wooden box when she thought about Mama. The face on the form was cold and gray. The body would never walk this earth. The preacher man said Mama was in heaven, living with God. "How could that be? "Thought, Hannah. Yet Mama lay before her. He also said Mama's spirit had returned to God, who gave it. Did she have a heart? She never saw Mama's spirit. Is a temperament like a ghost? Far as Hannah was concerned, grown up's had crazy ideas. Maybe a child wasn't supposed to understand grown-up things until they grew up.

Hannah thought she felt a gentle breeze on her shoulder. "Is that you, Mama? "She looked around her shoulder. She saw the tattered curtain, barely hanging onto the stick holding it up. The curtain did carry a few baby cobwebs. And a few bugs. She quickly pushed down the window and closed the curtain. Hannah laid her head on her arms on the window sill. "I want to go back to my real home in Germany," Most of all, I want my Mama back. Nothing could replace her. Salty tears ran down her cheeks, spilling into her arms and hands. She wiped her face with the dirty curtain. She managed a little smile; sorry, Mama. You don't want me to use a dirty rag to wipe my tears. Hannah felt a warm rush of comfort and peace. Hannah took a clean handkerchief out of her apron pocket, wiped her face, and said, "thank you, Mama, for listening to me. I hear your voice in my heart."

"HANNA RO ROSE ZIMMER, ARE YOU IN THERE?"

The voice and thundering footsteps came closer and louder. It was Sister Agnes, "Why is she yelling, and why is she in such a hurry?" thought Hannah.

The sounds of veils and black skirts waving in the wind and the clank of a chain belt with a cross and keys could only be one person.

Sister Agnes swooped into the room with a toddler in her grip. His tiny feet were moving so fast that he barely touched the floor.

"HANNAH' do you know who this is?" well-m, of course, I know who this is," said Hannah smiling and kneeling and taking the little boy's hands in hers.

"How are you, "Sam-Sam?"

"Sam – Sam," you say?" roared Sister Agnes in a loud voice. Have you forgotten that you and your Sister told me that you would take care of Samuel, and you have forgotten his real name?" "I am sorry, I get mixed up when I am nervous. Please forgive me," said Hannah.

"I forgive you," said Sister Agnus.

"Look at this little child, no more than a baby. What do you see?"

"We-well. I can see that he is cold, Hungary, and dirty."

"He probably found a mud puddle an-before Hannah could say more. Sister said that Samuel had been very naughty. He was throwing mud at everyone and trying to eat the dirt."

"Don'you feed this poor child?"

"Ah, um, he is good at throwing things. It is his favorite thing to do. You should see how he throws his food. We tried to get him to eat with a spoon, but he would rather throw it. If we feed him something he doesn't like, he takes it out of his mouth and rubs it in his hair or ours. I have seen him throw a biscuit as far as the next table. He laughs and laughs when he does these things."

"Why don't you have a lamp in here? How do you do homework and take care of yourselves in the dark? "Sister Agnus demanded. "Well, Sister Irene was walking by our room, and she saw Sam-Sam, excuse me, Samuel, throwing toys at the lamp. So she took it away because it was too dangerous. The room could catch on fire."

"So, Hannah rose, how do you and Lilly do your homework and get ready for bed?" inquired Sister Agnes.

"Lilly and I go down to the front hall and sit at a table with a lamp. We take Samuel with us. He plays with toys, runs around, and makes funny noises. Sometimes he takes his clothes off. He knows how to open the front door and throw toys on the porch. Sometimes other children will do it too. Sometimes it is hard for Lilly and me to get our homework finished. We take turns watching him while the others study. He is always tired when we put him to bed. We are tired too."

"No doubt about it, you have a lot of work to do," said Sister Agnes trying not l to smile. But now, the most important thing you have to do is give this child a warm bath, some clean nightclothes, and his supper."

"Sister Agnes," said Hannah, a little frightened," you have no idea how hard it is to bathe Samuel."

"I am sure you and Lilly will find a way to do it. But, remember, he is still a baby. So you have to start showing your authority with him."

"Sister, I have more questions about taking care of Samuel." "Make it fast." Said the Sister looking at her wristwatch. "Sister, he has accidents in his draws during the Night. The smells wake us up. Lilly and I closed our eyes or held our noses. We can't leave him like that. After we clean him up, he goes to sleep. We have asked him if he has to go to the toilet. I don't think he knows what we are talking about or what we mean. His dirty clothes smell up the room. We don't know where to put them. The laundry is too. Far away, at Night. We put the smelly clothes on the floor outside by the door."

"Why do you close your eyes to clean him up? Are you embarrassed because he is a little boy?" said Sister Agnes.

Hannah stood in front of Sister Agnes and looked at her face. "You don't understand. We have never taken care of a baby. We don't know how to toilet-train him. We try to keep him clean.

We never leave him except when we are in school. We have heard complaints from m the nursery worker—"I have listened to enough of your complaints!! I will ask Sister Catherine to arrange for the nursery nurses to advise you. She took a small pad of paper and a pencil out of her pocket, wrote on it, turned, and said, "One more thing." How do you get your homework done?"

"We take him to the front hall after dinner and sit at a table with a lamp. He is noisy and throws toys and balls. He knows how to unlock the front hall door. Soon all of the kids do it. Most toys end up on the front porch or the yard."

Sister Agnus walked away, muttering," Thank God for Sister Catherine."

"Don't worry, Sam, Lilly, and I will always care for you."

Hannah put the child on her lap and hugged him. Sam patted her face and laid his head on her shoulder. Lilly kissed his forehead "I hope supper is ready. Said Lilly. I am Hungary." "Me too," said Hannah.

Lilly opened a small box sitting against the wall. "I hope we have enough clothes to last Sam until tomorrow, said Lilly laughing. Sam pulled off his clothes and ran around the room with a pair of underdrawers on his head."

Hannah took out a 0ld1 trunk from under the bed. The girls brought it with them when they came to the orphanage.

The girls took out two tattered quilts. Hannah will wash Lilly's blank and wrap Sam in her quilt.

"Hannah, I just thought of something funny. These quilts look like Sam has already used them."

"He is rough on things, but we love him anyway." Said Hannah. No matter what mischief Sam gets into, he brings joy and laughter to the two young girls, the only mamas he knows.

"Hannah," do you think we should bathe Sam-Sam before or after supper?" inquired Lilly.

Both girls agreed; that they would have to clean up Sam once after supper. The girls filled a pillowcase with towels and rags and nightclothes and soap. They used an apron to tie him to his chair while eating and a wet cloth to wipe off the spills. The girls took turns carrying him piggyback. That was the best way to keep track of him.

Sister Agnus got to her office as fast as she could and hoped to find Sister Catherine at the desk.

"I am so glad you are here, Sister Catherine," said Sister Agnus.

"I will pour some tea. I think it is still warm." Said Sister Catherine pouring tea into a cup. What has upset you?"

"The little boy Samuel stays in the same room with the Zimmer girls, Hannah and Lilly."

"Oh yes," said Sister Catherine sipping her tea. "Was he rude or threw something at you."

'He is cute," admitted Sister Agnus; all children are cute in one way or another." Samuel likes to throw things, and I don't know why. The girls bragged that he could throw a biscuit from his table to another table. I think Hannah and Lilly were proud because he could throw that far. I believe there is another complaint about him."

"Do You mean the volunteer Miss Dorothy who helps the younger children while the older children are in school?"
"Yes," said Sister Agnus; she is the one."

"Sister Catherine, there is one more issue. Will you arrange for a nursery nurse to explain to the girls how to toilet-train Samuel? Maybe they have some diapers they can put on him at Night."

"Sister, I think you will feel better after supper. Let's go to the dining hall now,s" said Sister Catherine "I do know what is wrong with me, complained Sister Agnus. I am the oldest of ten children. I helped take care of them. I taught high school and grade school for several years. I did not realize how much work it is to help care for an orphanage. The building is old and needs repairs, And There are leaks in the roof. The front porch needs repair. There are broken windows. At times, I am afraid to open the front door. I am worried a needy child will be standing there with a note pinned to his shirt. Sometimes, a parent will bring their child inside to register them. The only discipline I know is talking in an authoritative voice. I don't think the children like me. Hannah Zimmer is not afraid of me. She boldly told me how hard it is to take care of Samul. I am glad I put him with the Zimmer girls. It takes a lot of work to care for him. I was going to send him to the boy's building. They said they didn't have room for another toddler."

THE VISITORS

CHAPTER 3

Papa's pocket watch no longer rested on Hannah's night table, reminding the girls it was time to get up, get ready for school and take care of Mama, who was very ill. Hannah put the timepiece into the darkness of old and useless rags, its final resting place in a closet in an old trunk. Hannah still helps Lilly prepare for school but misses caring for Mama and the pocket watch's rhythmic ticking. At one time, Mama took care of her and Lilly. Now it is Hanna's turn to take care of Lilly. She can still hear Mama's sweet singing voice, gentle touch, and goodnight kiss from both parents. The orphanage has taken all of those precious memories away. Her life seems useless as the cobwebs make a home on the ceiling wallpaper above her bed. She didn't understand the wall hanging on a cross from her bed. It was not raining at the moment, yet the ceiling was damp. She worried the roof and all would fall on top of her. The room above her is the bathroom where babes are bathed. Hannah knew when she washed Sam, a a lot of water spilled on the floor, then the floor leaked and came down on her ceiling, So that explained the leak—trying to bathe babies made sense that water would drip through the ceiling. One more thing to ask, Sister Catherine, how does she keep the roof from caving in on her? Hannah wanted to snuggle under her quilt, cover her head, and hide from her life's misery. The room was void of heat. The floor was old, cracked, dirty, and cold. She and Lilly found some old blankets and put them on the floor, especially near Sam Sam's crib. Both girls try to keep shoes and socks on him. They did not want splinters to get into his little feet or theirs. He thought it was a game to take off his shoes and clothes, throw them, and the girls retrieve them like an old hunting dog. Both girls had to work fast to dress him and hurry out the door before he could get into more mischief Hannah hated the new sound of the morning bell ringing loudly in the hallway, reminding everyone to get up, get dressed, gather homework and books, and get to the breakfast table on time. The soft ticking of Papa's watch was gone forever. She wasn't sure who wandered up and down the hall clanging a bell. She laughed to herself, picturing Sister Agnus waving her bell.

"Get up, Lilly, so that I can brush your hair. Are you going to wear it in braids or tie it back with a ribbon?"

"I will wear my hair in one braid without a bow." But, of course, the boys always untie it and run. Stupid boys!"

"I will braid the ribbon into your hair; no one can pull it out."
"Oh, that's" right," said Lilly sliding out of bed. What's that funny noise?"

"It's Sam, Sam, shaking his bed," laughed Hannah, oh! Oh! There he goes, climbing over the rail out of his crib." If he isn't throwing something, he is climbing in or out of something." Both girls giggled. Hannah picked him up and gave him a good morning kiss.

"Oh, NO!" said Hannah, quickly putting the toddler down on his feet. He is soaking wet! I must get him into dry clothes before he catches a cold. All we have is Coldwater in a pitcher. Lily, would you……"

"I know said Lilly yawing. So you want me to go to the kitchen and bring up a pan of warm water?"

"We can't clean him up in cold water. How would you like that?" said Hannah, taking the wet clothes off the shivering child. I will wrap him in a blanket to keep him warm until you return."
"Oh, banana nose; I was trying to look in his mouth to see if he had enough teeth to brush. He does! He bit two of my fingers! If

I see Sister Catherine, I will ask where we get a toothbrush for him."

"I am so glad Sister Catherine told us how to keep Sam in the room so he won't run away during the Night. We ALWAYS have to lock the DOOR and put a chair in front of it."

"I know that Lilly, quit talking and bring the warm water. We don't have much time, and I still have to find some dry clothes for this little rascal."

Hannah quickly dressed and tried to keep an eye on Sam. "Where is your other shoe, Samey?" Say shoe.

Soo!" Sam announced with expression and drooled down his adorable chin.

Little Sam, Sam crawled under his bed and smiled with the lost shoe, a few cobwebs, and a dust bunny or two. "Thank you, Sammy, say thank you!" said Hannah.

"YOU," said the child in a playful voice. "You know what, Sam, Sam, you are getting too big for these shoes. That is one reason you take them off all of the time. You poor little thing. You don't have a mama or a papa, and none of your clothes don't fit you, but we have each other!"

Hannah swung him up in the air to delightful giggles from a little orphaned boy. All anyone knew about the little fellow was his name on a cloth pinned to his tattered coat.

Hannah and Samuel heard a loud howling like hail pounding on the grimy window. Hannah looked out and saw trees bending in the wind. Whirlwinds of sand splattered on the old building. Hannah signed and said to Sam, at first, I thought it might be Sister Agnus howling up a storm!" But I guess it wasn't her howling on the rooftop this time."

Scorpio, on the cusp, was hurling warnings of impending storms, rain, or snow. Cold weather is coming to the Eastern Seaboard. Hannah shivered and held Sam, Sam closer to her. She wished they could have a rocking chair like the one at the end of the hall. While Hannah or Lilly read him by lamplight, Sammy loved to rock in the big chair. Both girls want a lamp; it could hang on the wall in their room. Doing homework or getting ready for bed in the dark is hard. Hannah heard Lilly at the door. She opened it and said, why were you running so fast? You are out of breath."

It was starting to rain, so I had to" walk fast. Don't worry.

There is enough warm water to clean up our little Sam, Sam." "The new girl Gwen from Scotland said she and her little sister Allison would save a place for us at their table. They have a brother about two years older than Sam. His name is Duff.

"I will carry Sam on my back to breakfast. He is getting too heavy to put over my shoulder and carry his pillow to sit on."

Hannah walked out the door, reminding Lilly to pick up the book bag, towel and apron so they could tie Samuel to a chair.

"Don't worry," said Lilly patting her dress's pocket. I have a cookie for Sam and Duff. I hope this will keep them quiet while we get their food.

"Yeah," said Lilly. Sam will throw his cookie, and we will run after it, and he will laugh. I think there is something wrong with this situation."

A wave from Gwen, Allison, and Duff indicated they had a table waiting as Hannah, Lilly, and Sam entered the dining hall. "Hi, everyone," was echoed by the two sisters and a louder."

HI" from noisy little Sam, Sam. He wanted down off Hannah's back to run to his friend Duff.

"They play well together," said Gwen," and Duff hasn't learned any bad habits from Samuel."

"Well, what does that mean?" Lilly said with her hands on her hips.

"I'm sorry," replied Gwen, it's just that Sam throws things and is loud; you know what I mean."

"Sam, Sam is a good boy. He is full of energy and loves to play with Duff.

"I didn't mean to start an argument or say anything mean about Sam. Let's get a table so all of us can have breakfast together. After getting the kids settled and eating breakfast, I have some news to tell you two."

"Lilly, would you and Allison mind sitting with the boys while getting some food? Remember the treats you have in your pocket."

"Don't worry, said Lilly, and I know how to take care of Sam and Duff. Hurry back! The children soon enjoyed the same breakfast they had every morning, hot oatmeal, biscuits, and sometimes fruit or juice-boiled eggs. There were more important things to think about than the same old breakfast.

"Ok," Gwen, let's hear about the vital information you heard in the kitchen," said Hannah, taking the biscuit.

Gwen daintily wiped her mouth with her apron and said, "Some visitors will soon be here, maybe by this weekend."

"What's so special about that? Said Lilly, slurping her milk; visitors come here all the time. They bring all the old stuff that no one can use, so they give it to us. Sometimes they give us candy and toys."

"I like the dresses and bonnets they bring chimed in Allison; they were here yesterday."

"I don't MEAN that kind of visitor, " said Gwen, angry. These visitors are from the railroad. I don't know if they are here to give rides or what they want. They are visitors from some children's help society and help look after poor children like us. A Rabbi from the Jewish orphanage not far from here will be with the other visitors."

"Who are they going to talk to?" Lilly, ridging with her apron. "I am guessing Sisters Agnus and Catherine and the other Sisters who help take care of us," said Gwen.

"Are they going to send children away on trains?" asked Hannah

"You mean those trains people get on, and you never see them again?" Lilly asked, full of fear.

"I think that is what takes place. They look at all the children and then put them on a train that goes out West, and no one ever sees them again, at least around here," said Gwen looking right into Lilly's worried little face.

"Gwen, what is a rabbi?" asked Lilly in a low voice. "What's a Rabbi?"

"He is a teacher at a Jewish synagogue, like the Catholics, have teachers called Father or Sister, or in the Lutheran or Presbyterian Church, he is called a pastor."

"Oh, one of those people!" said Lilly. I hope he doesn't want to take Samuel away from us, and I won't let anyone take him!" Lilly sobbed into her apron.

"There, my little Lilly, don't be afraid; maybe the Rabbi wants to meet Sam, Sam, and find out if he knows Hebrew words."

Hannah tried hard to console her little Sister. Yet, she felt the visitors could take Sam to a new home away from them.

Gwen suggests that the teacher may want to teach Sam about little Jewish boys."

"NO!" argued Lilly; he has to learn English like the rest of us!" Hannah gently wiped the tears from Lilly's face with her apron.

Just then, they heard a playful squeal. Sam, Sam had lightly rubbed red jam in his hair.

The girls laughed and said it was time to get the two little boys to the nursery for the day. Secretly Hannah worried that she couldn't concentrate on her lessons. She was as concerned about the visitors as Lilly.

When the children got to the nursery, they noticed a different girl was working their today.

"Hello, my name is Dorothy. Elsie will be away for a few days, and I am taking her place. I want to pin a name tag on each child so that I can remember their name."

"Gwen," you don't seem upset about these visitors." Hannah tried to ask so Lilly and Allison would not hear the conversation. "For Allison and Duff and myself, I think going on the train could be a chance for us to have a real home, parents, someone to sew pretty dresses, love us, and everything a family offers. Do you want to grow up in this place?"

"No," said Hannah, in a stern voice; the worst thing that could happen is we be separated. I cannot imagine life without Lilly and Sam. We used to have a big family in Germany, and then we came to America. All we had was Mama and Papa. That was ok. We had a pleasant time with Frau, Frau Bruno, and her three sons. Now, all we have is the three of us. I will fight it."

"You are braver than I am," said Gwen. So I'll race you to the classroom."

"Good morning," "Sisters Catherine and Grace. Are you on your way to a short meeting in the office of Sister Agnus?"

"Yes," said Sister Grace to Sister Catherine. We have a few more last-minute details to discuss before our visitors arrive. She is very thorough and does not want us to forget anything."

As the Sisters entered the office, Sister Agnus was already speaking. "Welcome, everyone. Thank you for being on time, and I apologize for the small space for our meeting. Unfortunately, some of you will have to stand up because there is no more room for chairs.

Sister Agnus looked small and frail behind her big wooden desk, but that didn't take away from her faithful service, work, and devotion to many homeless children.

"I have some papers for you to read. We will give them to our visitors. You will find children's names to travel on the train that goes out West and their room numbers and building on the pages. They need to know that building A is for the girls and building B is for them. Also, tell them why there are some mixtures of boys and girls in these buildings. For example, if a little boy came with an older sister, we would house them for a while in building A; separating the very young from older siblings is difficult. We have hundreds of children here, all homeless. A few are half-orphaned, meaning they have one parent, but the parent doesn't have the means to take proper care. Every time a child does leave for adoption, we have more little ones waiting on our doorstep. All of the orphanages are overcrowded. We care for these precious children and want them to have a home."

Our visitors will be our guests sometime between noon and the evening meal. They will stay for the Night. All children won't be here; some older ones have lunch at school. There will be children in the play yard, especially the younger ones. And you can take them to the nurseries. Ask them to mingle with as many children as possible.

As you know, finding the right child for the right family is essential. Please pray about your work and ask God to send the right children to suitable families. Make sure the visitors get a list of children.

Miss Emily Warner will be here on behalf of the railroad. She coordinates the train fare and schedule for the children. Miss Pauline Brown is from the Children's Aid Society of New York City.

Miss Pauline and her coworkers ride the train with the children and track how they adjust to their new family. We know there can be abuse; sometimes, the boys and girls are taken in as workers rather than family. Of course, children need to learn to help and do chores, but love comes first. Rabbi Eli will be here from the Jewish Orphanage a few blocks from our buildings. He has some vital information to share with all of us. I will see you at noon with our visitors if they arrive. May God richly bless you on the enormous task before all of us. God Bless!"

"I am so glad school is over today, and we can get Sam, Sam, out of the nursery and back to our room. I have been thinking of some ideas about these visitors," Hannah picked up their books. We have to hide so they don't see us."

"How will we do that?" said Lilly frowning. That will be hard to do.

"Don't worry about that now," said Hannah. The first thing we have to do is get Sam out of the nursery. He is a good boy. He does things in funny ways. But, unfortunately, the nursery lady acted like he was trouble."

"Hi," said Hannah and Lilly at the same time. "We are here to pick up Sam, Sam.

"Who," said Dorothy in a weary voice. "You know, the little boy named Samuel." "OH, HIM! "Said the tired nursery lady.

"He is not an HIM!" said Lilly angrily. He is a little boy!" "I am sorry," said Dorothy, it's just that he is so busy."

"Was he mean to the other children?" inquired Hannah.

"Well, no, he plays well with all of the kids; he does things. I opened a window to shake out some blankets, and before I knew it, Samuel was throwing toys out the window. Soon all of the children were throwing toys. I made them all go outside and get them and put them away. Samuel tried to throw them back thru the window. I don't know what happened to his shoes. He probably threw them away. I think they are too small and hurt his feet. You should get him some bigger ones.

"Here he comes, running across the room to meet you. My goodness, he has underdrawers on his head!"

"He doesn't wear that kind, he likes"………

"No matter!" said Dorothy. Please take him to his room or wherever he stays!"

Sam, Sam climbed into the arms of the ones who love him. Both girls gave him cuddles and kisses and said he could have a cookie before dinner.

"I just remember something Gwen told me while working in the kitchen," said Lilly. "There is a big bin where the clothes are stored as they come in. They are sorted and then taken to a closet. Let's look there for some shoes. Do you think he would like brown or black?"

"I don't think it matters," said Hannah. He doesn't know his colors yet. We need to find something that will fit."

"I have an idea said Hannah while sorting through the various dresses, skirts, and boys' clothes. Let's disguise ourselves; no one will know who we are."

"What does disguise mean?" asked Lilly.

"It is like putting on a costume to cover up ourselves.

"That will be fun," said Lilly looking for something to wear. Sam had a lot of fun burying himself deep in old clothes and shoes. The girls laughed when they saw his little face peeking out from the rummage.

The three children had fun trying on different clothes. Finally, they decided to dress Sam up like a little girl. He disliked the pink or lace bonnets but eventually settled for an old straw hat.

The girls were sure it had once belonged to a scarecrow. The girls piled their hair on their heads and dressed like boys.

"We had better get out of here before getting caught," suggested Hannah.

"You are right, Hannah, we don't want to miss dinner, and it is getting dark."

"Lilly, I just thought of another great idea." I have to work in the laundry on Saturday, and I think you have to work in the kitchen."

"Yes," said Lilly. We can take turns hiding Sam with us. I don't think the visitors will look in the kitchen except to eat. They would not be interested in the laundry. We can hide. Let's hurry to our room."

"Wait a minute said Hannah with caution. Some strangers are out in the front yard shaking hands and talking to each other." "Do they look like they are important?" said Lilly peeking out from behind the maple tree in the back of the yard.

"They do look important," said Hannah. The strangers have notebooks and pencils. Usual visitors don'. They dump stuff in the kitchen and the clothing bin. Let's try to spy on them and keep Sam quiet.

"I am so glad to know you, Rabbi Eli, my name is Pauline Brown from the Children's Aid Society, and this is Emily Warner from the Railroad. We met a few minutes ago."

"We haven't been to this orphanage in quite a while. The number of children is increasing, and they are running out of the room", said Pauline.

Miss Emily giggled and put her hand to her mouth. "Is something going on?" inquired the Rabbi.

"Yes," I see two children. I think girls dressed up like boys that keep peeking around the maple tree and younger children. I am not sure if it is a boy or a girl. When the young one looks around the tree, he's pulled back by the collar. Maybe they are afraid of being put on the train. Some children have great fear; they have never seen a train. We need to be very gentle and patient with these lost ones. My heart does go out to them." Let's go inside the dining hall. I can't help but laugh at their imagination."

"Let's go to the kitchen now and get our supper. Said Hannah. No one pays much attention; there are so "many kids," We can hurry and eat and get to our room. That way, we will not be noticed.

"Good idea, Lilly; let's get out of here. I hope Sam can run in his new shoes, which look too big. Maybe we can stuff them with something or put two pairs of socks on him."

"Another good idea, little sis, hurry. I will carry Sam if I have to. You grab the rest of our things."

"I'm glad we had supper a little early. I don; think anyone paid any attention to us," said Lilly, almost out of breath and glad to be back in their room.

"Let's get our hair brushed, and we can go down the hall, sit in the rocking chair by the lamp, and I will read you and Sam a story," said Hannah while looking for a storybook.

Let's get Sam cleaned up and into some nightclothes," said Hannah, looking in the baby's crib.

"Speaking of Sam," said Hannah in a panic. He is not in his crib. Instead, he must have climbed out, opened the door, and run away.

"We have to find him," said Lilly, now!"

You stay here, Lilly, while I go and get him. I have an idea where he went."

"I don't want to stay here alone," pleaded Lilly.

"You stay here in case Sam comes back before I do. You don't want Him to be here alone, do you?"

"I guess you are right. I will stand in the doorway so Sam can see me when he comes down the hall."

"Good girl!" I will be back as fast as I can".

"Hannah," I didn't think you and Sammy would ever get here. I was afraid. There was thunder and lightning and a lot of rain. I didn't like being alone.

There is one more thing that scares me. That is the train I hear every Night. It sounds like it is going to run into our room."

"How often do I have to tell you not to be afraid of that midnight train? It doesn't stop. It just keeps going to where ever it is going. It can't hurt you. Besides, the train has to run on a

track. There are no train tracks in the yard. So go to sleep, sweet little Sister.

Ask God to comfort you. Sam and I are right here. We are together."

THE DECISIONS

CHAPTER 4

Exhausted and spent on emotion, Sister Agnes struggled with the day's decisions.

Still at the table, she thought about each child on the train to a new life.

She could trust God that the committee had made the right decision and the children would have a new home and a life full of love. To experience true love was still overwhelming and exasperating to sister Agnes. She left herself venerable because she still feared love not returning. How could she fill the emptiness in her heart?

She was getting older; maybe she couldn't pour out true love, and her heart was empty.

She prayed for forgiveness. she observed Sister Catherine, with envy, gliding thru life. Sister Catherine never raised her voice or a hand when the children disobeyed. She never scolded in anger. The children seemed to want to be around the sister and tried to be obedient. Sister Catherine didn't have to remind everyone always be polite and mannerly. The children would follow her because she always had time for them. Sister Catherine even jumped rope with some little girls, played catch, and even played tag!

"Sister Catherine is young, that's it, " thought Sister Agnes." Her legs are still flexible and limber enough To run and play.

Deep down, Sister Agnes knew she never played with children. Instead, I scolded them or told them to run along and play. Sister Agnes heaved sad little sighs when she heard Sister Catherine talking and playing with the children.

"Sister Agnes, don't sit at the table worrying about today's decisions. Sister Catherine picked up the leftover paper pens. And folders We have to trust God to guide us and keep the children safe. Let me walk you to the rocking chair by the fire, and I will bring you another cup of hot green tea. I know you like to sit by a warm stove," said Sister Catherine with a sly smile.

Sister Agnes wrapped her shawl around her, walked to the chair, and settled in to rest briefly. Her many duties include bathing children, evening prayers, and homework.

"Sister Catherine, what just happened? asked Sister Agnes. in an irritated voice. I was drinking my tea, and then little Samuel came in like an explosion. Maybe he is too much for Hannah and Lilly to handle. Rabbi wants to send him West to California. Maybe we should consider that."

I will take you to your room, said Sister Catherine gently. You can have supper in peace. I can join you if you want company and prayer time."

"I don't know what I want, said Sister Agnes in a low, trembling voice. I need to get away from noisy children for a little while."

Hannah, Lilly, and Sam walked in silence to their room.

Samuel was quiet and sensed he had caused a disturbance. "Hannah asked Lilly. So do you think The Sisters take a bath?

They wear so many clothes, and maybe they don't get dirty. Where would they bathe if they did?"

"Lilly, why would you ask a stupid question like that? Adults don't let kids watch them take a bath. We have other things to think about, be quiet!"

"I am sorry, Lilly, I don't feel well. As soon as Sam has his bath, take him down to the lamp and stove and read him a story. I am going to bed now!

Lilly blinked her eyes and tearfully looked at her sister. Hannah had never yelled at her. She must not feel well. She loves to help care for Sam and read him stories.

"Don't worry; I will take care of Sam and check on you."

"Thank you, Lilly. I want to be left alone.

: Hannah, wake up; time to get ready for school, said Lilly in a cheerful voice. Sam was patting her on her face.

Hannah looked out from the covers at the two people she loved the most.

"Lilly, please find Sister Catherine. I don't feel well. Dress Sam, take him to breakfast, drop him off at the nursery, and go to school. I am not going to school today. Please don't ask me; find Sister Catherine, NOW! Hurry!"

Lilly did what was asked of her and quickly dressed Sam. She and Sam quietly went out the door. Hannah rubbed her back and belly. I hope Sister Catherine gets here soon. She will know what to do. Soon there was a knock at the door.

"Hannah, this is Sister Catherine. May I come in?"

"Yes, please come in," said Hannah pulling the covers around her shoulders

The Sister came in and quietly closed the door. "Hannah, what's the matter? How can I help you?"

She sat on the bed and took Hannah's hand

"I don't know for sure." Hannah moaned, turning on her side and facing the Sister.

"I have had a terrible accident and don't know what to do."

: Accident? Said Sister Catherine with concern and a slight frown on her face.

"Look said Hannah pulling back the covers

"Oh, dear said the Sister as she observed the red stains on Hanna's sheets and nightgown. You haven't had an accident. You have turned into a young woman. How old are you?"

"I am almost fifteen, sniffed Hannah. I sort of know what happened but not for sure."

"This is what we will do, said Sister Catherine helping Hannah out of bed. I will help you clean up, wear fresh clothes, and change your bed. First, I want to talk to you, and then we will go downstairs to see one of the nurses."

"Why do I have to see a nurse? Complained Hannah, am I sick?"

"No, you are not sick, said Sister Catherine, looking for some clothing for Hannah. The nurses are trained in these matters and can explain them to you better than I can. They have medical books, pamphlets, and other resources. They will ensure you have the proper undergarments, and you will know what to do next time it happens."

"Next time? Cried Hannah; this is going to happen AGAIN?" "Yes, Hannah, once a month until you are about the age of Sister Agnus. Then everything stops, and you don't have to go through this inconvenience every month. I add that you will be glad to get your cycle sometime in your life. The nurses will
discuss this with you."

"Does this happen to all of you all of the time? You are a nun, and_

"Yes," said Sister Catherine with an amusing smile; underneath these skirts and veils, I am a woman like you. It doesn't matter what clothing you wear; a woman is a woman all her life, even Sister Agnus."

Sit on the bed, and I will talk to you for a moment before we go downstairs to see a nurse.

Usually, a girl s mother helps her daughter at times like this. You don't have a mother. All of us women at this orphanage
understand this. Although we can never replace your mother, we help and guide you. I will explain some of the things that are happening to you. The nurse will have specific information on how the female body works, which will help you understand more."

"Think of this time in your life as a season. The splendor and tenderness of spring arrive early, ready- to receive the life before you. The farmer toils all day in the hot sun. He prepares his field to accept the tiny seeds he planted to thrive and rise into beautiful acres of green pastures. Meadows were bursting into delicate blossoms, ready to receive a graceful butterfly, a honey bee tending to her hive. The trees show off their blooms like a bouquet of fresh spring flowers. God provides the sun and rain to help cultivate His creation. Each season arrives in her fullness and beauty at the precise time set eons ago—the Loveliness 0f God's pregnant season with life is the freshness and perfection of God s plan to help summer give birth to autumn's beauty, and autumn gives birth to winter."

"All living things work and rest in their season and their kind. Finally is the winter season, the season of Sister Agnes. Even her hair is white like snow. Her body doesn't need to prepare for planting anymore. It is finished, and the task 0f cultivating and producing is over.

"We need to ensure she gets rest and doesn't have to worry about life. We want her season of rest to be rich with God's blessings and the wonders of His design for us.

"Now, let's go downstairs. While you are there, I will find you some clean sheets and a blanket. Have some breakfast. I am sure the nurse will help with the cramps. When you get time, talk to Lilly so she won't be surprised when it happens to her. Things are going to be okay. Your monthly cycle is part of growing up. Let Lilly ask the questions or bring up the subject."

"By the way, how is Samuel doing on his toilet training.?"

"The nurse Doris is so lovely. She knew what to do. He is learning how to ask when he has to use the toilet. Most of the time, he wakes up dry. I have one more question."

"What is it?" asked Sister Catherine.

"Sam Sam likes to play in the outhouse. We have to drag him out. Why would he do that? It is so disgusting!"

"Well said, Sister Catherine; why don't you ask Sam why he likes a stinky place like that?" Then she closed the door.

Hannah sat on her bed, deep in thought. " I Have never asked Sam why he does the crazy things. I must remember to ask Sister Catherine what season she is in. Probably early summer."

THE MIDNIGHT TRAIN
CHAPTER 5

Hannah woke up to the ringing of the irritating morning bell. She didn't know if the sound upset her or the person ringing it. She wished Papa's pocket watch was on her nightstand. It was quiet and accurate.

She heard a shaking and rattling sound. A pat on her shoulder told her Sam- Sam was up. She peeked out from under her pillow. There was Sam-Sam full of smiles and a little drool.

She and Lilly thought he might be cutting more teeth. Lilly learned not to open Sam's mouth and count his teeth. The girls decided they weren't sure how to teach him to brush his teeth. They knew he would throw the toothbrush and have them look for it like a dog fetches a bone. They decided they needed more than one toothbrush. The girls wanted to find one that wasn't used like everything else.

Hannah opened her covers, and Sam skillfully crawled under the warm blankets. Hannah could tell his little body was shivering, and his hands and feet felt ice cold. No wonder he was wet up to his neck. She quickly stripped off the damp nightclothes, wrapped him in a blanket, and put him under the covers.

"You stay here, Sam, while I find you something dry. I'm afraid you will catch a cold."

The child seemed to understand and snuggled under the warm, dry blankets.

"I suppose you want me to get some warm water from the kitchen," said Lilly in a sleepy voice.

"I'm sorry, Lilly, I don't know what else to do. This room is cold, the floor is full of splinters, and Sam doesn't know how to ask to go to the toilet. I don't know how to teach him those things."

"I don't remember how I learned, and I know I find the toilet when I have to go. Who do you think showed us all about going to the toilet and where to put the pee?" Lilly said while putting on her shoes and socks.

"I don't remember either," said Hannah, still searching the room for something dry to put on Samuel.

"Probably Mama or our grandmothers taught us. When we grow up, we will know all about those things. There is so much to learn about being grown up."

"We better get Sam taken care of first," said Hannah trying to dress Sam.

"That's right, when we grow up, we will know about many things," said Lilly on her way out the door. "Oh, by the way, banana nose, how will we know when we are grown up?"

"When I don't have to yell at you anymore. Sam can't wait that long, you silly Lilly. He needs to know now before he freezes to death. Hurry with the water!"

Hannah put Samuel on her lap and cuddled him. All of us need many things. How will we get them before we grow up?

Sam patted her face and laid his head on her shoulder.

"Don't worry, Sam, Lilly, and I will always care for you." She rocked him back and forth in her arms.

Lilly soon came into the room with a pan almost full of warm water. "I ran so fast I think I spilled some," she said with a grin.

"I will wipe him off enough to get rid of the pee smell and ensure his hands and face are clean," said Hannah. "Would you help me put on his shoes and socks? He takes them off as fast as I put them on."

"We will give him a bath tonight," said Lilly, trying to put a shoe on Sam's plump little foot.

"Hey, banana nose," said Lilly trying to comb Sam's hair, "did you know there are sticky lumps of wet stuff in his hair?"

"Yes," said Hannah with a giggle. "There is the red jam in his hair. I am sure more stuff will be in his hair before the end of the day. We will get it tonight when we bathe him."

Hannah picked up Sam, and Lilly picked up the rags and aprons bundle needed to tie Sam to a chair. They opened the door. The trio started down the long, dimly lit hallway to the dining hall. The entrance looked as tattered and old as some of the sisters hurrying to breakfast, thought Hannah, "Lilly, stop," said Hannah, putting her hand in front of Lilly to keep her from going further. "Look at the entrance to the dining hall. Who do you think is standing there talking to everyone as they go into breakfast?"

"Oh no," said Lilly, "do you think it's them?"

"Yes," said Hannah, hugging Sam a little tighter. "It's those visitors! That's a sneaky way to take Sam from us. You go up and talk to them while I hurry by with Sam. I hope Gwen found a table at the other end of the room. Go, Lilly! Think of something to say that takes a minute or two. Hurry!"

Lilly carried her bundle of aprons and bibs and boldly walked up to the visitors. She stopped and smiled at them while letting other children be ahead of her. Miss Emily saw Lilly and reached out her hand to greet her. Lilly backed away and said,

"Guten Morgen," and hurried past the visitors hoping they didn't understand German.

"Just a minute," said Miss Emily, "we haven't had a chance to talk to you."

Lilly wanted to say that was the idea, but she didn't. She knew she had to be polite.

"Are you here alone, or are you meeting someone?" asked Miss Pauline.

"Uh, I'm not sure yet," said Lilly nervously. "I always meet someone."

"That's nice," said Miss Pauline, "are you taking some things to your friends?"

"I don't know," said Lilly, "but if I see them, I will have everything."

"Well, BIS Morgen!" said Lilly.

Lilly calmly walked into the dining hall, looking for Hannah or Gwen. Soon she saw Hannah waving at her at the far end of the room. Lilly walked slowly and gracefully toward the table, hoping her bundle didn't come untied.

"You did a good job, Lilly," said Hannah, patting Lilly. "You gave me enough time. Gwen was already here. Now we can have breakfast."

"I don't know why you girls are so afraid of the visitors or the train," said Gwen. "They aren't here to grab you and take you away. It could be a good thing for all of us." Gwen patted Hannah's hand.

"Gwen, don't you know that we may never see each other again if we get on that train? We are all friends." Hannah put her face in her hands and tried not to cry.

"I know," said Gwen looking down at Allison and Duff. "These two little ones need a home, and I would like one also. A home with parents and a bedroom and a new dress. Wouldn't that be nice to have all of those things? I would live with a different family if I could be near Allison and Duff."

"That's not going to happen," snapped Hannah. "If they split you up, you stay that way. If you allow your brother and sister to stay with a different family than you, it would be so far away you would never find them. Even if you found them, that doesn't mean you could live with them or near them."

"That is not going to happen to us," said Hannah and Lilly in agreement.

"Hannah, Sam is not even your real brother, so why should it matter if he goes on the train and you and Lilly go somewhere else, as long as you have a home?"

"Gwen, you don't seem to understand. The Sisters gave Sam to Lilly and me when he first came here. We love him as much as you love Allison and Duff, and those old nuns will not take him away," said Hannah beginning to be irritated!

Hannah could tell she was starting to lose her temper. "I am sorry, Gwen; I didn't mean to scold you. It's just that sometimes things get hard to do. Hannah said with tears starting to run down her cheeks.

"Don't worry, Hannah," said Lilly, putting her arm around Hannah's shoulders.

"Let's not talk about it anymore," suggested Gwen. "We have some restless little children who might start running around if we don't get them some food. Oh, by the way," said Gwen with a smile, "I have a biscuit in my pocket for Sam to keep him busy until you get back with his breakfast. I will stay here with him."

"Thank you so much," said Lilly. "He is a handful, but we love him! We will hurry back with food. Don't forget to tie him in his chair."

"I don't think I will forget that," said Gwen. "Sam, do you like your biscuit?"

"Yes," said Sam, with food falling out of his mouth.

The three visitors stayed at the dining hall entrance for a few more minutes.

"I think all of the children must be in the room," said Rabbi Eli looking up and down the hall.

"This has been an interesting morning watching the children enter the room. My heart hurts knowing none of them have a real home," said Miss Pauline with tenderness.

"I agree," said Miss Emily. "We are the ones to find them a home."

"Oh look, here comes Sisters Agnus and Catherine," said the Rabbi. "Good morning, Sisters," said Eli, shaking their hands. "Do you think all of the children are here by now?"

"I hope so," said Sister Catherine.

"We have learned things about some of the children and their names and age," said Miss Pauline. "I will tell you more when we get to the breakfast table."

"I think we should divide into pairs or threes and sit on either side of the room," suggested Miss Pauline. That way, we can observe the children easier and talk to them. We should introduce ourselves gently. Sometimes children don't like to talk to strangers because they are shy or afraid."

"Good idea, Miss Pauline," said Sister Catherine. "You and the Rabbi can go with me to the left side toward the room's far end. I think I see a table near the Zimmer girls."

"Fine," said Sister Agnus. "The rest of us will go to the other side. I think a few more Sisters will be joining us. There is a bigger table down at the right end of the room. I am also expecting some priests from nearby parishes. They try to contact Catholic families interested in adopting one of these precious little ones."
"Don't forget," reminded Sister Agnus, "to go out outside and mingle with the children in the yard. Even though it is rainy, some older children like to go outside. You might look around the laundry room. Even though it is Sunday, the children are good about bringing wet clothes from the clotheslines and hanging them inside to dry. The laundry is never done. The Lord won't mind us doing some necessary work on Sunday."

"Now that we have our food, we can discuss what we know about the children. We all laughed when the Zimmer girls came to breakfast," said Miss Emily. "I am still giggling."

"What do you mean?" said Sister Catherine, sipping her tea. "I hope they were mannerly and politeee.d."

"It's nothing like that," said Miss Emily. "They do funny things trying to disguise themselves and hide from us.'

"I heard about some prank," said Rabbi Eli, putting sugar in his cereal. "A group of us were in the front yard yesterday, ready to enter the building when we heard giggles and someone running. Little faces were peeking at us from behind the big maple tree in the side yard. The two girls tried to dress up like boys, and the little boy dressed like a girl with the funniest straw hat. He loves that hat. Every time I see him, he is wearing it. The girls don't let him wear it in the dining room.

"Before breakfast," the Rabbi said, "we waited at the entrance of this room so we could greet the children as they came in. Hannah was carrying the baby, saw us, and ran away quickly. The other little girl had some bundle of rags, unsure what it was or why she had it, and tried to stall us so that the older girl could find a table as far away as possible. The younger girl was quite clever. She spoke to us in German and hurried into the room, probably to find her older sister. I am not quite sure why they would do this. What do you think, Sister Catherine? You know them better than we do."

"Yes," said Sister Catherine, leaning closer to the Rabbi. "When they first came here —"

"I am sorry," interrupted Sister Agnus, "we have more to talk about than the Zimmer girls and their situation. We have many children here, almost too many to keep track of similar stories. All of them are sad".

Sister Catherine and Rabbi Eli exchanged awkward glances and decided this was no longer the time or place to say anything.

"This is what I expect from everyone today," said the annoyed Sister Agnus, "including those not here with us. Please mingle and talk to the children. Take notes or whatever you have to do to come to the next meeting fully informed. Today is the last day of our meetings, and I want to discuss your final recommendations and choices for children on one of the next trains. You have until four o'clock. We will all gather at the long table and chairs to the right in the front hall as you come in. The supper is at six o'clock. After the meal will be bath time for many of the children. Sister Catherine, some of the other Sisters, and I check each room to be sure the children are in bed, and we also say our evening prayers with them. We must also alert those who like to run around after bedtime. I think you know what I mean. Sister Catherine."

Sister Catherine slightly nodded her head in agreement. "Sister Agnus, if I may say, children are —" said the RabbI but was cut off by Sister Agnus.

"I will see you at four o'clock," said Sister Agnus. "After breakfast, I will be in my office for a short time. So do not be late and be prepared!"

"I guess we have our instructions," said Sister Catherine in a low voice. We have work to do The group watched Sister Agnus excuse herself and leave the room. Her hollow footsteps could hear in the chilly hallway, her skirts, and veils flowing behind her. She decided not to turn and go to her office. There were other matters to consider, like matters of the heart.

Sister Agnus went downstairs to the front hall to ensure her instructions were followed. The table is ready with extra paper and pencils, chairs, and a lamp. She also asked the kitchen to serve tea to the guests. She liked her green tea at four pm.

She looked out the front window and decided to go outside. The fresh air would suit her, and she did not mind a little rain. She wrapped her shawl tighter around her shoulders but decided her clothing was substantial enough for the brief time she would

Be out in the yard. She chose an umbrella from the stand next to the massive front door. It, too, had seen better times.

She had trouble getting the doorknob to turn, and the door stuck when it finally let go. She sighed. Everything around here needs repairing. We have So few resources and so much to do. She pushed the door to make it open and went outside. She opened the umbrella and met with a breeze that she thought could make her airborne.

The black umbrella had seen better days too. Some of the spines are bent, and there was a large patch on one of the panels. Sister Agnus looked up toward the sky. December was bringing angry black clouds filled with rain and maybe snow later in the day. Soon it would be late afternoon.

Sister Agnus carefully stepped down from the porch into mud and rocks. She hung on to the feeble railing that was ready to collapse. She was concerned that her heavy shoes might break a weak board. And get stuck in the mud! Someone needs to repair these stairs and porches!

She decided to turn to the right of the yard. That is where she could hear and see the children playing. Maybe watching them would help her get out of the doldrums.

Sister found an old chair with crooked legs, leaning on the maple tree's trunk for support and a torn cushion to add to its charm. The naked tree branches wrestled the wind, scattering the leaves into delicate patterns of the past season's colors. Otherwise, all signs of summer had disappeared. The old tree prepared to receive its winter coat of snow.

While Sister Agnus watched the children play games, she thought about their resilience. Skies decorated in gray, accompanied by Scorpio's cold, did not affect the children's laughter or fun. Their clothing patches were a kaleidoscope of colors and shapes, blending with sleeves or pant legs too long or too short. Two little girls played with jump ropes, their small braids or curls bouncing up and down like raindrops splashing on

An old water barrel. Boys were chasing girls. Girls were chasing boys. Some of the children were playing tag; some children were playing catch. A few toddlers and other young children were busy stompings in mud puddles. Most of them had never known their parents or where they came from. Yet, they thrived. What is their secret?

Sister Agnus began to think it was the cry of her heart, sad and terrified, too damaged to receive love. No matter how she tried to love, there was never enough room to plant the loveliness of love inside her fragile heart. Was it possible that she was hurt by past bruises and disappointments that love could not find her? What if she dared to love? Will it be returned?

After all, she let Hannah and Lilly have the roommate they wanted. She tried not to remember that it was for her convenience and the orphanage. Babies and toddlers were a lot to care for. They were busy, curious, and cranky and needed constant attention.

She looked at all of the dear children again. She was amused when children would act afraid of her or run like spiders when they saw her coming toward them. That Hannah Zimmer certainly did not run. She stood her ground. Sister Agnus heard her name called.

She looked up through a tear and saw some ragged children saying, "Hi, Sister Agnus."

She nodded slightly and managed to wave to them. These poor little urchins don't have much as material things are concerned. So how do they feel love returned to them?

She saw two children that she had scolded a few times. They didn't seem to mind her presence and even went out of their way to say hello. She thought of the words of the Good Shepherd Himself. "Look at the lilies of the field. They neither spin nor toil, yet I take care of them." Could that also include Sister Agnus, a Children's Orphanage administrator in New York City? Was it possible that she was a Lilly?

She knew right then and there what she had to do. She had to go directly to her prayer chamber. She remembered the psalmist's words, "Create a clean heart and a steadfast spirit in me."

Sister Catherine said her goodbyes and excused herself from the visiting group. She had so many things to do that day. First, she thought she would stop by Sister Agnus's office and look for more files. That office was partly hers, with at least one small file cabinet. She needed more space.

But like everything else at the orphanage, there was no room for another office, not even a closet, and if she did acquire an office, where would she find a desk and other supplies?

She was deeply thinking about her day when she heard a familiar voice. "Sister Catherine," hey Sister Catherine," and a squeal and laughter.

She looked up and saw Hannah and Lilly coming down the hallway. Sam broke from their grip and was running at full speed. She knelt with open arms to catch the whirlwind steaming toward her. Sam slid into her arms and laid his head on her shoulder.

He looked up at her and said, "Sis." She looked into the deep brown eyes and perfect face for a moment and drank in an innocent child's exquisiteness.

She laughed at his comical behavior,

"What are you children doing here?" She saw Lilly with a paper and pencil and Hannah holding a ragtag blanket, probably Sam's

"Sister, we need your help."

"Yes," said Hannah, "we have to talk to you now!"

"Is there anything wrong? Are you sick or in trouble?" enquired Sister Catherine.

"Oh, it's nothing like that," said Hannah. "We have to ask you to help us with something."

"Children," I don't have time right now —" She caught herself and said, "Okay, how can I help you? We can go into the office of Sister Agnus. I am going that way myself."

"No," said Hannah and Lilly together. "We want to go downstairs to the front hall and sit by the big window near the stove."

It will be warmer and more comfortable for Sam," said Hannah taking Sam by his hand.

"Okay," said Sister Catherine. "I don't have much time, but I am interested in what you have to say."

The four of them walked down the stairs to the front hall. It was cozier and warmer, with the potbelly stove doing its job, keeping the room more heated than the rest of the cold rooms.

Hannah wrapped a worn blanket around Sam and cradled him on her lap. Lilly took crackers from her pocket and gave them to Sam. Hannah kissed him on his forehead. Lilly patted his hand.

Sister Catherine looked at the trio and swallowed tears. They love that little boy and take good care of him. But she could not imagine what they wanted to talk about.

"All right, children, what do you want me to help you with? I have my paper and pencil ready. I see that you have yours."

"Well, the first thing," said Lilly looking at Hannah, "Sam-Sam does not have a toothbrush."

Sister Catherine breathed a small sigh of relief.

'You see," said Hannah, "mama and papa said we are not to share a toothbrush with someone else. It is not very clean, you know."

"Yeah," chimed in Lilly, "we have been looking for one, but we can't find a new one. Also, how do we show him how to brush his teeth? He will probably play with the toothbrush or throw it away, and we will have to find it or get another one."

"I'm sure we can get Samuel a toothbrush," said Sister Catherine, writing a note on her paper. "Is that all you need?"

"No!" said Lilly. "We are just starting."

Sister Catherine got a larger piece of paper and said, "I'm ready to listen to what else you need."

"Well." Hannah hugged Sam a little tighter. "He wets all over himself, and you know, the other. We try to clean up Sam the best we can. Sometimes he wears boy's underdrawers, but he wets those. We have found some diapers, but we don't know how to keep them on him. We wrap a lot of old rags and towels on him, but he takes them off and throws them around the room."

"I am sure all of that bulk is uncomfortable, and if his skin is chapped and sore, he does what we would do, take it off. No one like to wear uncomfortable clothing, and he is no different." Sister Catherine wrote more intensely on her pad of paper.

"How do we teach him to go to the toilet, and how does he know to tell us so we can take him?" said Lilly, waving her hands. The nursery nurses are helpful. Sam won't always do what we ask him.

"Oh dear," said Sister Catherine. "No one has helped you with this problem?"

"No!" said Hannah. "He wakes up in the middle of the night, cold and wet. We put him in dry clothes, but his bed is wet. It smells bad."

"So we put him in our bed and wrapped him in more blankets to keep him warm. It's not his fault."

"Of course, it is not his fault," said Sister Catherine while writing notes.

"The thing that breaks my heart said Hannah, on the verge of tears. "He gets sores on his legs, and it hurts and stings. We have a little ointment and salve that were Mama's, but we are almost out of it. Mama and grandmother used to warm blankets behind the stove and wrap us in them on cold nights."

"Yes,' said Lilly. "Sometimes, at night, I sneak down the hall before Sister Agnus finds me and put the blanket on the stove to get it warm. By the time I get back, it is not very warm. Poor Sam-Sam."

"I am so glad you girls brought this to my attention. I am also so sorry that you have this burden. There are so many children and so few staff. Some children get overlooked, like Samuel. You have done the right thing by reporting this to me. We want Samuel to be healthy and happy." Sister Catherine took a moment to write more notes on her paper.

"We have about fifteen nurses', excellent nurses, on our staff. Some of them are baby nurses. They are unique and know a lot about childcare. They know how to teach young children to use the toilet. We don't expect you to do that. You are doing an excellent job, and I thank you. Does Sam seem like he has a cold or cough? If so, tell the nurse. They have their office and medicine room in the basement. Also, they have all kinds of bandages, ointments, and salves. I will show you tomorrow where that is. If either of you has a scratch or other problem, they are there to take care of you. Is there anything else I need to know?" said Sister Catherine, giving the girls her full attention.

Sister Catherine interrupted before the girls could answer, "I noticed Samuel's little shoes."

"Yes," said Lilly, with a proud smile. "We found two brown shoes for him."

"Let me take a look at them," said Sister Catherine. She took both of his feet in her hands.

"See the left shoe?" Sister asked. "It has four holes for the shoelace and is low cut below the ankle. Look at the other shoe. It has more holes and is higher. These two shoes do not match. I think that is why he takes them off because they are uncomfortable. We would take off our shoes if they didn't fit properly."

"Anyway," giggled Lilly, "both are brown."

"That is true," said Sister Catherine, smiling and writing even faster.

"Sister, he needs better clothes; he grows out of his shoes, clothes, and crib. He can climb out of his crib, so we must keep the bedroom door locked. He can unlock the door, so we have to hang a chair on the doorknob and….."

"I am sorry to interrupt you, Lilly," said Sister Catherine with concern. "You keep saying you are looking for clothing, a toothbrush, and other things. Where are you looking for these things?"

"We look in all of the clothing bins," said Hannah. "There are several outsides near the laundry and even a room of old clothes in the basement."

"You mean you can open the door and get into all of these bins or buildings?" said Sister Catherine with concern. "How do you get inside without an adult or permission? They are to keep the door locked at all times. There should be a DO NOT ENTER sign, or a Do NOT ENTER WITHOUT PERMISSION sign. Sister Agnus very sticks to these rules. Someone could get hurt or locked inside. I will have to report this to her and find a helper. Did you see any signs on the ground or somewhere else?" "Well," said the girls simultaneously, looking at each other.

"We did see some signs on the ground, but we didn't pay attention because they were not on the door."

"We are sorry," said Hannah. "We didn't know we were not supposed to get into the clothing bins. Does this mean we will be in trouble with Sister Agnus scolding and yelling at us?"

"Don't worry about this, children. You have done nothing wrong. You were trying to take care of Samuel'. You did the best that you could. We are supposed to have volunteers who sort the clothes, mend them and wash them. The finished garments go into the large closet in the front hall. Many of these items are used in sewing classes so girls can learn to repair and make clothing themselves."

"That's what I want to do," said Lilly enthusiastically. "I wanted to bake bread in the kitchen, but all I get to do is scrub vegetables and wash dishes."

"I'm sorry to hear that," said Sister Catherine concentrating on her long list of notes. "Have we talked about everything you wanted to talk about?"

"Yes," said Lilly. "If we think of anything more, we will find you and talk."

"Goodbye, for now, children. I have to meet at four o'clock with Sister Agnus and our visitors. I will come to your room, say goodnight, and pray evening prayers."

Hannah and Lilly returned to their room with the sleeping Samuel. Sister Catherine decided to go to the office of Sister Agnus. She hoped she was there because there were many things to discuss.

Dressed in polished oak, garnished with brass and other metals, the old grandfather clock in the front hall, keeping track of moments of the day with his hands and announcing the time at quarter past the hour as well as half past and quarter to the hour and recording the hour of births and deaths and blissful times in the orphanage. Young children loved to look up at Mister Clock's face to tell what time it was while a graceful pendulum glided back and forth to the rhythmic sounds of tick-tock.

Sister Agnus came into the room when the clock announced four o'clock. No one was at the table. She walked to the table, put down her papers and notes, and tried to hold back annoyed and impatient emotions because the others were late. She did not tolerate late or those who didn't respect the rules.

She heard a pleasant voice saying, "Good afternoon, Sister Agnus."

She saw Gwen coming toward the table with a tray covered with a clean white towel. She could hear the clatter of teacups and saucers.

"Hello, Sister Agnus. My name is Junie. I haven't been here very long. Gwen asked me to help her with the tea." She was holding a fat pot of tea clothed in a tea cozy. "Where would you like me to put this hot tea?"

Sister Agnus looked at the petite nine-year-old girl with honey-blond hair woven into thick braids tied in blue ribbons.

Her little face was sprinkled with freckles and framed a smile that revealed missing teeth.

"Well, on the table, of course, in the center so everyone can reach it," barked Sister Agnus.

"Junie and I baked the cookies for you," said Gwen proudly. "Thank you. Don't forget we need a lamp; it is almost dark here."

"Right away, Sister," said Gwen. "We will hurry."

The girls looked at each other, wondering if they had annoyed Sister Agnus. They left the room.

Sister Agnus sat down and poured herself a steaming cup of green tea. She wished there was fresh lemon on the tray, but she knew that wouldn't happen in the middle of winter.

Sister Agnes took out her notes and began reading them. She was interrupted by Mister Clock, letting her know it was quarter past four. Her anger was kindled because she wanted to start at four o'clock; everyone sat down and got out of their notes.

"Thank you for coming to this final meeting," began Sister Agnus. "I hope you have concentrated on your assessments and recommendations. We are already half an hour into the evening. We have to cover everything, even if we are late for supper. So let's get busy and get our job finished."

The reliable oak clock reminded everyone that it was now time for supper.

Sister Agnus asked everyone, "Have you gone over your final notes and made choices that will benefit the children?"

Everyone nodded yes and looked at each other, hoping they had made the wisest decision. The Choices are final.

Hannah and Lilly were in the front hall doing homework when they heard noises outside. They ran out to find out what was going on.

"Look, Lilly, at all the carriages in front of Building B. Another one is coming, and it seems like it is pulling in front of our building A." Look at all the women carrying babies wrapped in quilts; some ladies have shoulder bags.

"I see a horse pulling a wagon of boxes and bags. They are probably clothes and food for the babies," exclaimed Hannah.

"Are you taking babies to a train station?" Lilly asked a carriage driver.

"Yes said the man, all of the babies are going on a train to their new homes in nearby states such as Pennsylvania, Michigan, and other nearby places. Even New York City."

"Is this your last trip for a while?"Asked Hannah. "No, there will be more baby trains until winter.

"The trains travel with the children in spring, summer, and fall."

"older children like the two of you go west to Oregon and California.

"Hannah," said Lilly in a low voice. I hear a train, and it sounds like it is coming here."

"Lilly, don't be silly. A train can't come here because there are no tracks near us. That's why people have to go to the train station by carriage." Go back to sleep and quit worrying about things. Winter is coming, so we won't have to worry about the train until spring."

MEETING DAVID

CHAPTER 6

"Hurry up, Lilly and Sam, " said Hannah while combing Sam's hair. "We don't want to be late for breakfast. We will eat with Gwen, her little sister Allison and her little brother Duff.

Hannah, Lilly, and Sam entered the dining room. They could see Gwen and Allison waving at the room's far end.

"Hi, everyone," said Hannah and Lilly while pulling out chairs.

"Why are you carrying a pillowcase and a pillow.?" enquired Gwen.

"Just watch," said Lilly putting a pillow on a chair, and Hannah put Sam on the pillow. Hannah tied Sam onto the chair and pushed it to the table. Hannah folded the towel into a bib for Sam.

"Now, Sam, you can have your cookie, " said Lilly, reaching into her pocket.

"Can Duff have a cookie?" asked Hannah.

"After breakfast," said Gwen, " we will get our breakfast. Would you watch Duff for a few minutes? Allison and I will get him some cereal."

"Yes, " said Hannah, " will you keep an eye on Sam while Lilly and I get his breakfast.?"

Just then, Sam threw part of his cookie at Lilly.

"Does he throw stuff all the time?" asked Gwen staring at Sam.

"Yes said Hannah and Lilly at the same time. He likes to throw things."

While eating breakfast, Allison asked if everyone had signed up for Laundry, kitchen, or yard work. I help in the nursery, read stories and pick up toys. I have seen Sam throw toys."

"I signed up for the kitchen. Added Lilly. I want to learn to bake like Grandfather Zimmer.

"I don't think you will get to cook announced Gwen. I know you will wash dishes and peel vegetables because I started in the kitchen. Then I worked in the yard and raked leaves."

"I like to work in the laundry, it's heavy, but the time goes by fast," indicated Hannah.

It was lunchtime at the orphanage school. Gwen, Lilly, and Hannah were eating their lunch on the school playground when Allison ran toward them with exciting news "What's going on?" said Gwen with curiosity. "Yeah, said Lilly, we want to get in on the fun too."

"Well said, Allison, out of breath; remember the message board in the front hallway?". I forgot to look for messages, but I looked today".

Allison sat down and munched on her cookie. "What did the message say? Asked Hannah 'The message said several ladies living near here volunteer to teach us girls who live here how to sew and make our clothes and knitting, embroidery, and crocheting."

"I want to make scarves, mittens, caps for Allison and Duff, and maybe something for myself," said Gwen.

"Hannah, what do you want to sign up for?" asked Lilly.

"I don't know for sure, Replied Hannah. I want to learn how to plant flowers and vegetables and care for animals, especially horses. I want to learn to harness and saddle them, drive a carriage, and ride a horse. It will be fun to learn to sew too."

The four girls, Hannah and Lilly, Gwen, and Allison, had decided to meet in the front hall the next day to walk to their respective sewing classes.

"Gwen and Allison are late!" said Lilly impatiently, twirling in a circle.

"I see them," said Hannah."

'We finally got here," said Gwen, out of breath. I had to make sure someone would look after Duff."

"Oh, I see you brought Sam. Wouldn't anyone look after him?" said Gwen laughing.

"Sam is coming with us!" said Hannah in a cross voice. Lilly and I don't see him all day, and we miss him." She pulled Sam closer to her and put her arm around him "Let's get going on our adventure," said Allison, happily skipping ahead of everyone.

"Hannah, I hate to say it," said Gwen cautiously, but Sam does many strange and crazy things.

'Then DON'T Say it!" said Hannah angrily. Come on, Sam, let's walk ahead of these girls!"

"Lilly, why is Hannah so upset?" asked Gwen.

"I don't know," said Lilly; something is bothering her."

Let's go and sign up now," suggested Gwen gathering her books and papers.

The girls, including Sam to the message board located in the dimly lit front hallway "Oh, I want to sign up with Miss Naomi Kilmore," Lilly wrote her and Hannah's names in the space provided for signatures.

'Why do you want her class?" asked Hanna, yawning and holding onto Sam's hand.

: I want her class, said Lilly because she has a sewing machine, and I want to learn to sew on a machine. It is faster and holds the stitches tight. It says Miss Kilmore works out of her home making dresses for women and girls and custom wedding gowns and formals. She also owns a dress shop in the city. Our first class will be on Tuesdays and Thursdays. I am glad tomorrow is Tuesday."

Gwen and Allison hoped they hadn't upset Hannah.

As the girls and Sam crossed the dusty street, they said goodbye and saw you at supper.

Sam said NO! with a big smile.

"Hannah, why does Sam say NO to everything?" asked Lilly. "I think it is his favorite word; he hears it so much. Remember how he got yes and no mixed up, and what way to shake his head? I think he is adorable, and I love the two of you more than anything," said Hannah, squeezing Sam's hand.

"We better hurry and look for twelve Rosehill road."

"I see Lilly pointing to a brick house across the dusty road. It is beautiful and has a carriage house attached to the home side". "I want to see the carriage," said Hannah pulling away from Lilly and Sam. Someday I will own and drive a carriage like that with my horse." Hannah, gazing at the polished black leather seats. I wonder where they keep the horse?" she thought Hannah.

Miss Naomi's house was next to several homes in a row on the block. They all looked like they were on an island with a dusty street on three sides and a barn and animals in the back.

As the girls approached the elegant home, they saw two long windows with two panes of glass, one above the other framed with gleaming white wood, in a neat row with the front door in the middle of the windows. Above, there were three more double windows in a .row. Dormers decorated the roof and assisted with fireplace chimneys on either side. A long porch stretched across The front of the house is supported with white spindle railings and narrow pillars holding up the triangular-shaped low rooftop to keep the rain off visiting guests.

The children walked up the brick path that guided them to the porch. The heavy front door with a long frosted glass window and a brass doorknob completed the look. A sign said to ring the buzzer before entering. Hannah lifted Sam so he could ring the buzzer. The children waited a few moments and heard light footsteps approaching the door. A beautiful young woman with auburn hair piled on top of her head secured with a jeweled comb. A few curls are draped on the side of her forehead.

The flickering oil lamp hanging from the ceiling in the foyer gave her porcelain skin the shade of a pale pink rose. Her delicate look was completed with beautiful brown eyes and a narrow nose, and Her cotton shirt with peaks of lace around the high collar added elegance. Puffed sleeves from her shoulder to elbow tapered into a slim fit to her wrist. The flickering oil lamp hanging from the ceiling in the foyer gave her porcelain skin the shade of a pale pink rose. Beautiful brown eyes, a long narrow nose, and almost heart-shaped lips complimented her face.

"Hello, children. I am Miss Naomi. Are you here for sewing classes?"

"Yes," said Hannah and Lilly.
And a loud YES!" from Samuel

"You must be the Zimmer girls from the orphanage?" enquired Miss Naomi.

"Yes," said Sam answering for the girls.

"Welcome. and come into my home. Please take off your overshoes, hang your hats and coats on the hooks by the mirror, then go into the room to your left and sit down. I will be back in a minute; I have something in the oven."

Miss Naomi turned and left the room. Her skirts made a swishing sound.

"Smells like cookies," said Lilly.

"Cookie?" said Sam.

Thick woolen scattered rugs in colorful red and ivory patterns covered glossy wooden floors. The parlor greeted guests with wallpaper embossed with silver and gold leaf patterns. Silky Victorian sofas and chairs stood next to glass oil lamps, giving the room a warm welcome glow. The unusual fireplace crowded itself into the wall, only revealing the glowing embers in its belly. Above the fireplace is a varnished heavy wooden mantel decorated with silver candlesticks. A tapestry in swirls of color rested above the mantel. Oil paintings are meticulously hung in the room, giving a look of artistry throughout the home. Heavy ivory raw silk drapes complimented the double windows.

The three children quietly walked into the beautiful room, not quite believing where they were. They hurried to the nearest silken sofa and sat down. Hannah decided to hold Sam on her lap. "We can't let Sam get away." Said Lilly, laughing. We would have trouble finding him in here."

Sam sat on Hannah's lap but had to go to the bathroom. He asked several times "What's that?" pointing to lamps, pictures, and the fireplace.

Sam struggled out of Hanna's grip and ran to the fireplace, "Hot!" he said, pointing his finger and shaking his head no. "I am glad he knows the fireplace is hot," said Hannah guiding Sam to the sofa and onto her lap.

"Thank you, girls and little boy, for waiting," said Miss Naomi returning from the kitchen and carrying a tray of warm oatmeal cookies.'

"Thank you, yes," said Sam taking a cookie with Hanna'shelp. "You are welcome," said Naomi with a smile "I need a napkin for Sam. He can make a lot of crumbs," said Hannah "Take one off the tray." Suggested Miss Naomi.

"Look at Sam, said Naomi. Laughing, he wipes not only his hands and face but also his hair."

"Sam always wipes his hands off in his hair," said Lilly giggling "Before you girls leave today, I need to put some information in my book. I want to track whether you are sewing or knitting, what you want to make, and the yarn colors.

"I know what I want to make," said Lilly taking another cookie. Tell me what you are interested in, Lilly," Naomi opened her notebook.

"I want to learn to knit, embroidery, and learn how to sew on the sewing machine," explained Lilly.

"Hannah, what would you like to learn," said Miss Naomi writing in her notebook" Well said, Hannah. I want to learn to harness and saddle horses and drive a carriage like the one bedside your house. Where do you keep the horse that pulls the carriage?"

"My nephew David and I own the livery stable a few blocks from here. Grandfather Kilmoore owns the horse Danny Boy David takes care of the horses, and I do the bookkeeping. David is studying to be an animal doctor."

"The horse is a beautiful black three-year od. Maybe you will meet David, and he can tell you about the horse and carriage. David lived in one of The bunkhouses. But I talked him into moving in with me. He does the chores, and I do the cooking. We take care of each other."

"We had better get to work, or class time will be over before we know it," said Miss Naomi

"I am showing you my sewing room. That is where we will do most of our projects."

"I think we have done enough for one day," said Miss Naomi putting, some notes and reading material in a bag for each girl. Sam played well with the toys. He loves the toy cat. I made the toy from scraps of a fur coat I remodeled for a lady. I never throw away anything. You can always make something out of a scrap of material."

I will help you get Sam bundled up, said Miss Naomi. She was leading the children to the foyer.

"Sam certainly wears colorful clothing," said Mis Naomi while putting Sam's red scarf around his neck. I like this lovely green stocking cap, one brown mitten, and .one black mitten."

'Sam grows out of everything fast," said Lilly, putting on her overshoes. Sometimes He doesn't even fit in his crib; he has outgrown that too', giggled Lilly.

"Well, I think Sam is very handsome in all three colors," said Miss Naomi smiling at Samm and wiping crumbs from his mouth with her lace handkerchief.

"I hear my nephew David coming in thru the back door."

A six-foot-tall young man wearing a brown winter coat and a black stocking hat entered the foyer. Are these the children you want me to walk back to the orphanage?" asked David, looking at Hannah.

"Yes, said Miss Naomi, I want you to meet Miss Hannah Zimmer and her younger sister Miss Lilly and Samuel."

"Girls, I want to introduce you to my nephew David Kilmore.

His mother, Nora, was my older sister.

"Oh. Oh, said Lilly looking at Sam. He is pointing at himself. He does that when he has to go to the toilet. Is it out back?"

"What does he want?" Added David with a grin.

David and Miss Naomi looked at each other, trying not to laugh.

"No, said David, it's in the house."

"Oh, you mean a chamber jar?" said Lilly, embarrassed.

'No, Said David, is better than that. Auntie will show you where it is."

"I am going with Sam and Lilly," I don't want to miss this," said Hannah.

"Follow me," said Miss Naomi.

She led the children down a lit hallway with a small oil lamp that hung from the ceiling.

"There it is, " said Miss Naomi, an indoor flush toilet."

"What is that"? said Sam, looking at the porcelain throne.

"I will stay here and help Sam," Said Hannah. I take him to the outhouse all of the time but never to an indoor outhouse."

"When he finishes, pull the chain to flush it. He can wash his hands in the sink and use the towel to dry his hands."

In a few minutes, Hannah and Sam came out of the bathroom. Sam was all smiles and wanted to go back in and pull the chain. "No, Sam said, Hannah, we have to go home; it's supper time." The children said goodbye to Miss Naomi. They walked with David in the cold and snow to the familiar warmth of the orphanage and their home. David and Hannah exchanged smiles as David turned and walked toward his home.

He looked back over his shoulder and said, "goodnight."

DRIVING DANNY BOY

CHAPTER 7

"**M**onday will be a lot of fun," said Lilly tying her shoelaces. "The best part of the day will be riding in Miss Naomi's horse carriage pulled by Danny Boy," said Lilly, and David will be there also. Don't you love it?

Then a lock of hair falls on his forehead, above his right eye, and those thick long lashes?"

"Lilly," I think you are more interested in David than the carriage ride."

"Hannah, banana nose, you know David is cute. You have said it many times. Maybe you have a crush on him," Lilly said, looking in the mirror.

"Miss Naomi said we are going to a department store to buy lace and ribbon for the bride's dress she is making, and we get to have lunch in a cafe. Hannah, have we ever been to a cafe?" said Lilly while looking out the window of their room to see if David was on his way. I don't think so said Hannah. But, Sam, I want you to be a good boy, don't run in the hallway. Keep hold of Lilly and my hands."

"Hey, banana nose," shouted Lilly, "don't forget your bag full of stuff for Sam. I have my bag on my shoulder." I will open the door for all of us."

"Thank you, Silly Lilly," said Hannah grabbing her large bag and adjusting the strap on her shoulder" Please don't call me banana nose. It is beginning to annoy me."

The two girls stepped into the hallway with a firm grip on Sam.

"Oh no," said Lily, "Sister Agnes is walking towards us." Sam let go of the girl's hands and ran into Sister Agnes. "Hi, Sis," said the small boy with a big smile.

Sister Agnes looked down at the child through her specials and said, "Hello, Samuel," please don't run in the hallway."

"Ok, sis," said Sam, waiting for the girls to catch up to him. "I hope we haven't kept David and Miss Naomi waiting," said Hannah, as the three children tiptoed down the long hall and carefully walked down the stairs with a firm hold on Sam.

Soon they were in the front hall and out on the porch. The wind of November reminded the children it was almost winter.

"I see them coming," said Lilly, jumping up and down. "He is so handsome and muscular!" said Hannah.

"I love his hair, said Lilly.

Hannah and Lilly looked at each other and started laughing. "Who are you talking about, Lilly?" asked Hannah.

"I am talking about David!" said Lilly with a laugh.

"I am talking about Danny Boy," said Hannah, hugging her sister.

The shiny carriage pulled by Danny Boy parked in front of the girls. David swiftly jumped down from the driver's platform with an athlete's skill.

"The carriage looks different," said Hannah. "Is it the same one that is always by Miss Naomie's house?"

"Yes," said David. "It is cold today, so I put the top on to keep all of you warm." Hannah loved the variety of hats that David wore. Today he was wearing a woolen newsboy cap perched on his head. The lock of hair that wouldn't stay in place draped on his forehead added to his adorable face.

David opened the carriage door. Miss Naomi slid across the seat and said, "good morning, girls and Sam."

"Hi, sis," said Sam waving his hand" Sam will sit in the middle of the seat, and Lilly, you will sit on the other side."I will put your purse on the floor. It will be safe here," said Miss Naomi tucking the little bag by the seat.

"Hannah, what do you have in that big bag of yours?" said Miss Naomi with her sunny smile.

"Well," said Hannah opening up her bag, "I have extra underdrawers for Sam," He has accidents if I don't get him to the toilet on time, extra socks because he might stomp in a puddle, and an extra pair of mittens. I have a cookie and a cracker wrapped up in a napkin, toy bear, blanket, and other things he may need. She took a cover out of the bag and gave it to Miss Naomi. "Put this across his knees. I don't want him to get cold."

"I brought extra blankets also," said Miss Naomi. Now, where do I sit?" asked Hannah.

"Hannah," I have a surprise for you," said David in his soft, masculine voice. "You are going to drive Danny Boy today."

"Does Danny Boy know this?" said Hannah with a smile. "Yes," said David. Danny is aware when there is a new driver.

He feels the tension on the reins. New drivers are often nervous, pull too hard, or keep the same stress on each reign. I am here to help you. Danny is a good horse and obedient. Have fun." Hannah," said Miss Naomi. I also have something for you." She reached into her purse and took out a pair of leather gloves. These driving gloves are for you. The reins are coarse and stiff and may put sores on your bare hands."

Lilly was beginning to get upset and feel left out. It must be Hannah's banana day, she thought to herself. She gets to sit by David all day. I get a runny nose and a cookie-crumbling little boy named Sam Sam.

"Come here, Hannah, and I will help you up to the driver's platform," said David. He climbed up first, then turned around and extended his hand to Hannah. She gracefully got up in one leap and sat beside David on the bench seat.

"Hannah, get ready, and I will hand you the reins," said David. "I am nervous," Hannah said, pulling on the gloves.

"I want you to hold a rein in each hand and keep a light steady tension. Danny Boy will do the rest of the work. Give the reins a little tap that will give Danny the signal it's time to go."

"I don't understand how Danny knows all the signals," Hannah said, trying to keep the reins secure.

"Remember, Hannah, I showed you the bit in his mouth. So when he feels it turn, he knows you want to go right or left."

"The big question, David, is, how do I stop this big boy?"
"Excellent question," said David, steadying the right rein. "

Pull back, and he will stop. But, on the other hand, don't pull too hard, or he will back up."

"That would be my luck," said Hannah, "if you see me driving a carriage down the street going backward, you will know it is me."

"Danny Boy knows the streets well. He has made a lot of trips to the city and all of the stores. Go straight. We will make a right turn after a few blocks. I will show you how to guide Danny. He may start turning before you do."

"Does Miss Naomi know how to drive a carriage?" asked Hannah, afraid to take her eyes off the road. "Yes," said David, she is a good driver. She knows how to put the harness on and take it off the horse. There is a lot to learn. The harness is secure, and it is fastened to the carriage. Naomi is so tiny and of a delicate size that I do it for her. She doesn't like to get dirty and knows I will take care of it. Danny knows all of the dress shops in town. So when auntie has the reins, he knows he is going dress or fabric shopping."

"Come on, Danny," said David laughing, take us through a mud puddle so Sam can have some fun."

Sam looked around where he was sitting. Not much to see. The top of the carriage didn't have much to offer. The doors weren't unusual. He couldn't reach the door handles. He crawled onto Lilly's lap to look out the window. "Samy." Do you see the dogs, horses, and a man pushing a cart along the board sidewalk?" "Yes," said the little boy pointing his finger. "Sam looks at the tall buildings. Maybe one is a candy store or a cookie store." Said

Lilly. I bet the cookie store smells good. He saw all the things he wanted to see, then crawled up into Miss Naomi's lap. "Sam," said Naomi adjusting him on her lap and looking at the water. That's the ocean. Maybe we will see a boat" The carriage bumped along, splashing in mud puddles. Sam squealed with delight when the muddy water sprayed on the windows.

Hannah sat silently, in deep thought. A breeze tickled her nose. "What are you thinking about?" said David, making sure the reins were steady. Is Central Park near here? asked Hannah, brushing a strand of hair out of her eye."It's not too far away, said David. Why do you ask?"

"One of the last times Lilly and I saw papa was in Central Park. He told us we were going on a picnic, and the5n we would get ice cream." He told us we had to live in an orphanage because he could no longer care for us. Mama died a month or so before that. Papa said he would visit us but has never come back. We don't know if papa is alive or not. He could be in heaven with mama. Our neighbor, Mrs. Bruno, helped papa find the orphanage. She never came to see us. We lived in a tenement house someplace in German Town. David, do you know where that is?" "Yes, I think I do. I know the city pretty well, especially the shops that auntie likes to go to," "After mama passed away, Lilly and I used to skip school and go to the park with other kids that didn't have parents. Some of them lived in shacks and got into trouble." "Your papa did you a favor by finding shelter for you and Lilly," said David. "I know that," said Hannah. I wish I knew what happened to him. Maybe someday I will find him." "I will help you," said David."Lilly and Sam, we are almost to the cafe," said Naomi looking out the carriage window.

"I'm hungry," said Lilly. "What kind of food do they have in a cafe?"

"I think you will find something all of you like. Soups, sandwiches, and desserts are on the menu. "You can choose anything you want," answered Naomi.

"I think I will have two desserts," said Lilly. We can only have one dessert. Sometimes there are not any desserts at the orphanage. Sam, what kind of a treat would you like?" said Lilly patting Sam on his knees.

"Cookies," said Sam.

"We just turned the corner. The cafe is at the end of the block. It will be fun to see how well Hannah brings the horse and carriage to a stop and in the right place," said Naomi, still looking out the carriage window.

"I am sure David will show her what to do. She always does everything right," said Lilly with a sigh.

"Hannah," ease up on the reins, then guide him with the left reign kind and gentle," said David giving Hannah and Danny Boy a bit of assistance.

"He is doing it!" Hannah said, almost out of breath. "Danny Boy is turning and going where I want him to go!"

"Pull back a little so that he will know you want him to stop. Don't pull too hard and put him in reverse," teased David. You did it, Hannah. Now tell him to stop Hannah gently pulled back on the reins, and Danny Boy came to a stop.

"Good girl Hannah. I knew you could do it, and so did Danny boy. He can get a drink of water from the horse trough, and I will give him some hay while waiting for us."

"David, what do horses do while waiting for people?" inquired Hannah." "They will do what most other horses do on this block: sleep. Remember, I told you horses and cattle sleep while standing? Now, let's open the doors for our passengers and go get some lunch."

David got off the right side of the carriage to open the door for his aunt. But, before he could assist Hannah, she too got off the platform and opened the door for Lilly. Lilly was disappointed when she saw her sister's smiling face at the door. "Did you have a good ride Lilly?" did you notice I brought Danny to a complete stop on the right street?"

"Yes," Hannah, you did everything just perfectly, like you always do."

"Come here, Sam, let me help you down the carriage step," Hannah told Sam. "Did you have fun?"

"Yes!" fun ride!" exclaimed the little boy.

David came around the corner of the carriage to ensure his passengers were safely on the ground. "Come here, Sam," said David, carefully picking up Sam. "Do you want to thank Danny for the fun ride?" Sam nodded his head yes. Sam gave Danny a pet and scratched his ears. "He loves that said David. Sam leaned over and kissed the horse.

"Sam, I think Danny boy should have a snack," said David while searching his coat pocket for a lump of sugar. "Let's take your mitten off so you can feed him the treat. Hold your hand flat and your fingers like mine," said David adjusting the boy's hand. Now hold your hand full of sugar under Danny's mouth."
Sam squealed and laughed. "It tickles!"

"Can you feel his lips and whiskers?" said David smiling at Sam.

"Yes," said Sam.

"Oh no," said Lilly with her hands over her mouth. "It looks like egg whites coming out of the horse's mouth."

Sam looked at it, too, and put his hand under the slobber to catch a handful. He looked at it with glee and rubbed it in his hair before David could get his handkerchief out of his back pocket or Hannah could find a cloth in her bag.

"Let's get him to the water trough and wash his hands," said David, trying not to laugh.

He carried little Sam to the water trough, knelt, and tried to wash off the drool. Hannah was busy getting it out of his hair.

"It is cold out here," said David looking at Sam, "I don't want to put water in his hair. We can fix him up at the café."

"That's all I need," said Hannah, laughing, to bring Sam back to the orphanage with icicles in his hair. Sister Agnes will come after me for sure."

Lilly stood back from the scene with her handkerchief over her mouth. Watching nearby, Naomi tried not to laugh at David, and Hannah was scrubbing Sam to get him clean enough to go into the café.

Hannah and David laughed while cleaning up Sam. David wiggled the stocking cap back on Sam's head while Hannah brushed off the mittens and pulled them over his hands. "I don't want Sam to get cold," said Hannah while looking in her bag for a cover.

"Let me wrap him up." David put the tattered blanket around the little boy's shoulders. He picked up the child and held him close to his chest.

David could feel the baby relaxing in his arms. Finally, David secured his hold on Sam, and he rested his head on David's shoulder.

"I will carry him to the Café," said David hugging and rubbing Sam's back.

"He is an arm full to carry," said Hannah patting Sam on his head.

"He is a pleasure to hold," replied David.

Lilly and Miss Naomi walked a few feet behind the trio and watched every move they made. Lilly hated it when Hannah and David looked at each other and laughed, their warm breath embracing the cold air. David had his hand on Hannah's elbow, guiding her. Lilly walked a little faster so she could hear the conversation.

Miss Naomi did not miss anything that was going on. What a lovely couple, she thought to herself. However, she could sense that Lilly was jealous and uncomfortable.

"Come here, Lilly." Naomi pulled Lilly to her side. "I know you have a slight crush on David, and I think David has a crush on Hannah. He hasn't taken his eyes off of her since we started on this outing "Hannah always gets what she wants!" fumed Lilly ."Come on, Lilly, don't blame your sister. I have not seen her flirt with David. She is devoted to little Samuel and takes good care of him. David is too old for you. Let's have fun. We are almost at the café. Do you see that small square building painted white with a large sign called "Jordens Sandwich Shop and Café."? That's where we are going. for lunch," Lilly still wanted to know what Banana Nose and David were saying.

"David," said Hannah, why does Danny drool so much?" I can remember papa and grandfather feeding the calves. They drooled. "Danny has drooled a lot since he was born. He never outgrew it. Our animal doctor said his saliva glands get overstimulated, especially when he eats sugar or an apple." I think Danny drools just for Sam."

"Now," said David, I have a question for you. Why does Sam rub everything in his hair?"

"I have thought about that," said Hannah, looking at Sam. I get after him for wiping his muddy hands on his clothes, and believe me; it is hard to keep Sam clean, so he rubs his hand in

his hair. I think he is wise to think of that. I love him so much. I often think of him as my little son. Lilly loves him too."

"Here we are at the café." David jumped off the driver's seat and opened the café door for Hannah and Sam. He waited for Naomi and Lilly to catch up with him.

The smell of fried chicken, apple pie, and other tasty things greeted the guests.

Lilly looked at the polished wooden floor, the beautiful embossed wallpaper, and the criss-cross curtains at the windows. A potbelly stove, warm and cozy, added to the room's warmth.

David carefully set Sam down and said, "wake up, Sam, it's time for lunch." Sam opened his eyes and said hi, "Davdid."

"David, I think you have a new nickname, said Hannah kneeling and taking off Sam's coat, hat, scarf, and mittens. She hung them on the coat rack, standing by the door.

Sam whispered in Hannah's ear.

"Oh," ok, I will take you. Naomi, do you know if they have an outside toilet or an inside one? You never know these days. I hope it is inside."

David said, "I know where it is. I will take him'"

Before Hannah could protest, David took Sam by the hand and walked down the hallway.

Lilly told everyone this café was her kind of place, and she could eat there daily. She would curl her hair and wear a party dress."

Miss Naomi pulled off her leather gloves and walked over to a long walnut counter, and said, "hello," Mr. Jordan, how are you today?" A mature man turned around in his swivel chair, adjusted his glasses, and said, "hello," Miss Kilmer I didn't" expects you today. Our granddaughter, Mary Beth, said you and some guests would join us for lunch today. Welcome." Mr. Jordan stood up, adjusted his vest and bow tie, and asked, who are these two charming young ladies?" "Walter, I want you to meet two good friends, Miss Hannah Zimmer and her younger sister Lilly

Zimmer." Where is David? Did he come with you?" asked Mr. Jordan." Yes,' said Naomi. He is helping another friend named Samuel. They will be here any minute."

everyone could hear laughter, a squeal of amusement, and " want to pull the chain again!" Is that Samuel?" said Walter chuckling at the sound of a small boy. "Yes, said Hannah. Sam always makes noise and likes to explore and get into things."

"Here is Mary Beth," said Mr. Jordan. She will take good care of you. Enjoy your lunch. We have a full menu today, things I hope the children will like."

He sat down behind the counter and continued his paperwork. Hannah and Lilly looked at one another. "Who is the child, you or me?" said Lilly.

David and Sam came out of the bathroom and joined the ladies.

"Look," said Sam, holding up his hands," All clean" He patted his damp hair, and it was clean, too." "Don't put your hands in your hair, Sam; it is still wet," said David.

"Ok," Davidid," said Sam.

"Hannah," He had fun pulling the chain and watching the water go down. I didn't know if I would get him out of there without your help," said David.

"David," David Kilmore, is that you?" David turned around and saw a young girl with bouncing blond curls approaching him. David, it's been a long since we have seen each other." She gave him a hug and a kiss on the cheek.

"Oh, I wish Hannah could see this, " Lilly thought. She looked around the room and saw Hannah and Naomi admiring a painting.

"Is that you, Betsy?" I mean Mary Beth, said David. "Do you work here all of the time?" I thought you were at nursing school up north somewhere."

"Yes," said Betsy, "I am helping my grandparents run the café for a few months. Then, in January, I will go back to school."

Mary Beth picked up a menu from the counter and said to David, "How many are here with you today?"

"My aunt Naomi, my friends Hannah and Lilly, and a little boy named Samuel. He is running around here somewhere."

"I do like this painting Hannah," said Naomi. "I love pictures of horses and scenes from out West. I think our table is ready."

Hannah lingered and wondered what is it like out west. "Hello," Miss Naomi," said Mary Beth, "so lovely to see you today." "Please follow me," Mary Beth said to the group. I will seat you by the big windows, so you have something to look at."

"Betsy," said Hannah, do you have a high chair for Sam? These chairs are too big for him."

"Yes," What did you say your name is?" asked Betsy. "My name is Hannah, and I need a high chair for this little boy named Sam." "Yes," replied Betsy, I will get it for you. Small children don't come in here very much."

"You will know Sam is here," said David picking up Sam.

"I think Sam will be more comfortable at the end of the table," said Hannah. "Lilly, you can sit by David near the window. Miss Naomi and I will sit on the other side.

Lilly was hoping to get into a conversation with David, but he talked to Hannah. Lilly decided she would have a good time.

After lunch, everyone went shopping, and Lilly wanted to go to a fancy dress shop. Little did she know she would be shopping without David and Hannah.

JIGGIDY JIG
CHAPTER 8

Naomi sat at her kitchen table, enjoying another cup of tea. She finished the papers she would ask David to take to Sister Agnes. "hi, Auntie." Said David coming through the back door. "I was thinking about you. Said Naomi. Would you please deliver these papers to the Sisters?" There is more planning for the upcoming Christmas party for the orphanages. I told Sister Agnes, you would bring them to her."

"Take Rung with you," said Naomi walking over to the fuzzy black and white shepherd puppy. "I love his name," said Naomi leaning over to pet the dog. The white ring of fur around his neck looks like a collar. "Would you like a cup of tea?" I need to talk to you about some things."

" Thank you, Auntie" you know I am a coffee drinker." "I have some coffee on the stove."

"just finished writing the invitations to be posted in building A and B's front hall."

David looked at the papers while slurping his coffee. "I forgot there would be a Christmas party for some of the local orphanages at the old Atlantic Side Hotel." "How many kids from each building?" asked David.

"Twenty-six from each building," replied Naomi. I chose an even number because I didn't want any children to feel left out.

"There are other parties in the city for the orphans, but this is the one I like to work on."

David kept looking at the papers while he drank his coffee. "I saved a meat bone for Ring. Is it ok if I give it to him? He will have to go outside with it."

"Yes," said David, half listening. "Put him outside; he can chew on something besides my boots."

"What have you been doing this morning David?" you seem a little lost."

"Nothing new." I got up early and did some studying. I graduate from veterinary school in June and must pass the final exams to get my medical license. So I did my chores and had breakfast with Ring. I took him outside, threw snowballs, and he tried to catch them."

"David," I think you are lonely," said Naomi taking off her apron and smoothing her hair. "Why don't you invite Hannah to the party with you? "She is lovely, and I think you like her."

"You are right, auntie. How do you know that I like her?"

"We women have ways of knowing the heart of a man. "I think she likes you too."

"Well," said David, since I have to go over there anyway, I may invite her." "What if she says no? What should I do?"

"There he is, Lilly and Betsy." They love it when you talk to them." Said Naomi with a smile.

"NO!" not those girls!" Lilly is a little girl, and Betsy is a flirt and aggressive, "Hannah is my type."

"Before you leave, I want to give you something." Naomi opened a cupboard door and took out a small box tied with a pink a ribbon on a cloth bag. "Hannah will love this German chocolate" There are lollypops in the bag for Sam." Said Naomi. " When Hannah accepts your invitation, the first thing she will worry about besides Lilly and Sam, what will she wear?" I will help her with that."

"You have all of the answers, auntie," said David. "I have the heart of a woman," said Naomi playfully. Go see Hannah and invite her to the party."

"I am on my way," said David tucking the envelope of invitations and the candy in his coat pockets.

Naomi watched David leave from the front window. She could hear him whistling and talking to Danny Boy. I wonder what he says to Danny? Thought Naomi

Lilly, Junie, Gwen, and Allison were doing homework in the front hall. Junie heard someone out in front. She ran to the window. "Guess who is here?" said Junie; it is someone all would like to see."

"Is it David?" said Lilly running to the window. Gwen followed behind Lilly. "I think he is holding a present tied with a pink ribbon," said Gwen.

"Oh," it is David," said Junie. "He is dreamy," "He is here to see Hannah," said Lilly.

David walked up the front steps, opened the door, and said, "Hi" to the girls.

Lilly ran to David, "Are you here to see Hannah?"

"I have to give some papers to the Sisters," said David. "I would like to see Hannah. Is she here?"

"Yes," said Lilly. "She is in bed reading to Sam. She doesn't feel very well."

"Oh." Said, David. I hope she is ok."

"She is ok," said Lilly; she is in her season."

Junie and Gwen fell over each other, laughing. "Lilly," you did it again, speaking before you think," said Gwen

"I am going up to see her," said David walking towards the stairs.

"Boys" aren't allowed upstairs near the girl's rooms," informed Junie.

"A boy isn't going up there," said David with a twinkle in his eye.

"The room is number twenty-two on the left at the top of the stairs," said Lilly trying to hide her embarrassment David's long legs allowed him to take two stairs at a time. When he got to the top, he saw Hannah's door was open. He looked at the young woman and child that would become important in his life.

HANNAH

Hannah propped up with pillows, and Sam curled next to her and turned the storybook pages.

David peaked into the room," anyone home?"

Hannah looked up and said, "David, what are you doing here?" Sam scrambled off the bed and jumped into David's waiting arms. Sam kept a tight hold on David's neck and laid his head on David's shoulder.

"Auntie asked me to deliver some papers to Sisters Agnes and Catherine. It will take a few minutes. I want to talk to you about something after seeing them." May I take Sam with me?"

"I don't think you will get away from him," said Hannah trying to pull the covers around her.

"Oh," by the way," said David standing in the doorway, cuddling Sam, "I hear you are in season?" I have a mare in season. Is that the same thing?"

"OH. NO!" screeched Hannah, throwing a pillow at David and hiding under the covers.

"Anna," mad," said Sam. Don't throw that!" He said, shaking his head no.

"See" you in a few minutes Hannah," said David with a teasing laugh. We better get out of here. Sam or Hannah will get after us."

Hannah got out of bed, found something to wear, and brushed her hair. She wanted to look nice when David came back. She was excited to hear what he had to say.

David and Sam walked down the hall to the office of Sister Agnes. He knocked on the door and heard the announcement to" come in." David opened the door. "Good morning," said Sister Catherine. We have been expecting you,"

"Hi, Sis," said Sam.

"Hi yourself," said Sister Catherine with a smile, patting Sam on his hand.

"I have some papers for you from Auntie," said David. He put Sam on the floor and took a large envelope from his coat pocket. "Auntie has written the date and time for the party. We will bring enough sleds or carriages to take the children to the Atlantic Side

Hotel". The local merchants are donating food and toys for this event. The City of New York has many generous citizens.", said David.

"David" is the Atlantic Side one of the remodeled hotels near the waterfront?" asked Sister Agnes, smiling and looking well.

"Yes," said David picking up Sam. It has electric lights, several rooms for parties, a large dining room, and a café. Many of the big stores downtown also have electricity. Today I will take Hannah and Sam to see some stores and Christmas decorations." Hannah worries about Sam because he has never had anything new. Today he will get his first pair of new shoes and a new toy."

"That is generous of you," said Sister Catherine.

"I was looking at Samuel. He reminded me of you when you were about his age". Said Sister Agnes. "You were one of my first students and best student."

"You were one of my favorite teachers," said David. "You taught me many things. If auntie needs to talk to you, she will come over, or I will bring the message." So, goodbye, Sister Agnes and Sister Catherine," said David smiling and hugging Sam.

"Bye, sis," said Sam waving at the two women.

David quietly closed the door and walked toward Hannah's room. "Let's get Hannah and go for a carriage ride. Do you want to pet Danny Boy?" said David, looking at Sam's little face.

"Yes," said Sam. I want to pet Danny and get candy."

"David knocked on the door of Hannah's room. "May we come in?" said David, still wanting to tease Hannah.

"You can come in if you have candy," said Hannah. "We have candy," said David walking into the room.

"Candy?" said Sam trying to get into David's shirt pockets.

David took a bag with a pink ribbon out of his pocket and handed it to Hannah. She untied the ribbon, opened the bag, and said, "German Chocolate!" my favorite!" She took out a piece of chocolate and said: "This is the c best candy ever!."

"I have lollypops for Sam." Said David, handing her the bag. She untied it and told Sam he could have one lollypop. Soon he was licking the lollypop. Streams of sticky goo were running down his chin and onto his shirt.

"It is clean-up time," said David trying to wipe Sam's chin with his handkerchief.

Hannah's face was rosy pink and still blushing. David looked at the young woman that God sent to him. She was standing in a ray of sunlight dancing through the window. Her beauty and pure heart made him love her more. This young woman is the one he is going to marry. Together they would raise a large family, starting with a precious angel named Samuel.

"How long will we be gone?" said Hannah, looking through the giant bag full of Sam's clothes.

"I am not sure. Do you have to be back at a certain time?" said David.

"No," said Hannah laughing. I want to be sure I have enough dry clothes for Samy."

"Good idea," said David admiring the little boy in his arms.

David carrying Sam and following Hannah, walked downstairs into the front hall.

"Lilly," said Hannah, I will be gone for a while. I get to drive Danny Boy."

"Ok," said Lilly looking at Hannah. Before Lilly could say anything, Hannah told her not to worry and was not mad at her. "I love you, banana nose," said Lilly. "I love you, Willy," said Hannah. The sisters hug each other.

"We know Sam will come back in different clothes," laughed Junie and Gwen.

Don't worry," said David. We have a bag full of towels and clothes.

The girls ran to the window and watched the three walk to the carriage. David, holding Sam let him pet Danny, then got on the platform first. He extended his hand to Hannah. She gracefully stepped up, sat down, put on her driving gloves, and picked up the reigns. Let's go, Danny Boy," said Hannah. "By the way, David," where are we going?"

Holding Sam on his lap, David said, "We are going to the city. Some of the big department stores have electric lights and

Christmas decorations. I thought it would be fun to take Sam to a toy store and buy him a new one. Then, we can go to a children's clothing store for his new shoes."

"I love that idea," said Hannah.

"I have another idea," said David. " We are going to have lunch at the Atlantic Side Hotel." It is one of the historic hotels that has been remodeled and has electricity. I want to invite you and Sam to a Christmas party with me at the hotel.". Auntie and her friends help sponsor Christmas parties for many children in nearby orphanages. The party is the Saturday before Christmas, about two weeks from today."

"I love parties,", especially at a grand hotel," said Hannah with her hand on her chest. "I don't know what I would wear; my hair is always a mess; Sam would need several changes of clothes…..I don't think Lilly has a party dress. She has grown out of most of her good clothes; my clothes don't always fit her_."

"Hannah," said David snuggling close to her and putting his arm around her shoulder, you don't have to worry about that. "Auntie and her friends help the girls with a dress and messy hair."

"Do you mean it?" said Hannah looking at David. "I don't want special treatment; that wouldn't be fair to the other girls. " They like party dresses, and hair do's as much as I do."

"Hannah," said David kissing her on the cheek. "Auntie owns a dress shop and makes custom party clothes. Her friends do the same thing. There are enough girls in town to keep them busy all year. So let them have fun getting all of you girls ready for the party."

'That sounds like fun," I can hardly wait for the party," Sam will look cute dressed up, clean, and in new shoes." "thank you, David; you make me happy," said Hannah, smiling at David.

Hannah enjoyed driving Danny Boy, especially with David at her side. However, Danny is not in a hurry. Sometimes he goes through mud puddles or a bump.

Hannah drove along sylvan fields decorated with naked trees waiting for spring to clothe them with their fresh new blossoms.

HANNAH

Now that she has become a woman, she is in a season of new beginnings. It became clear to her; that being poor had no power over her—a young man Loved her, And a child provided contentment and happiness. In her heart, she said, "Father, thank you…."

The New York City skyline was not far away. Suspicious clouds of snow or rain lingered over tall skyscrapers. With tears, she remembered Papa saying, while their ship from Germany entered the New York harbor, "see the city that is American, our new home and new life."

Hannah recalls nightmares of her first years in America. No longer are their ghost and grotesque faces of the night. Now there is rest, the restless sunset races to the early sunrise, and the daily grim is hope and promises from God.

Hannah's daydream was interrupted by the left reign having no tension. "David," I think something is wrong with the left rein; it is to lose." David said," I thought I tightened that strap. Stop Danny, and I will guide him to the side of the road". David jumped down from the platform and went to the horse's left side. Sam woke up suddenly and wanted to follow David. "Sam, you sit here by Hannah and stay there!"

"Okay, Davdid," said the small boy.

Hannah leaned over to talk to David and ask if she could help. Sam was sitting still when he heard barking dogs running and playing in a field. They were doing something strange. Sam tried to get Hannah's attention by pulling on her coat sleeve. "Annah," dogs were jumping on each other, then he laughed and clapped his hands. "Anna," doggie is ridding the other dog."

Hannah finally looked over her shoulder to see what Sam was looking at. "OH," NO!" Sam, you sit down and don't look at them!"

"What are they doing, Hannah?"

"AH- well, I don't know, "they are playing jiggity jig." "Jiggy?" said Sam.

"Yes," said Hannah, the dogs don't want you to look at them." "Jiggy dogs are funny," said Sam.

David knew what was happening and could hardly wait to hear how Hannah would explain this. Hannah could feel her face turning several shades of red. She knew David was going to tease her. David returned to the platform, brushed off his clothes, and said, "what is Sam looking at?"

Hannah put her head in her hands and tried not to look at David. Sam kept saying," dogs. Funny."

" Hannah," you can tell me what the dogs were doing."

Hannah pulled her scarf around her face, leaned over, and whispered what she told Sam to David.

"SO THAT S WHAT THEY CALL IT!" David laughed so hard it startled Sam.

David and Hannah were laughing in each other's arms, and Sam started to laugh. Sam kept trying to look back and find the jiggy dogs. David found a cracker to keep Sam busy until they got to the hotel.

"David." Do you know the address of the hotel?" Said Hannah, not wanting to look at David. She knew she would blush or start to laugh.

"Yes," said David, somewhere off of Broadway and Spring. Auntie said we should see the sign that says Atlantic Side Hotel. There is a place across the street for Danny; he is ready for water and a treat." December's icy fingers stirred up dirt, paper, and debris. Hannah covered her face to keep out the odors of horses, hay, and garbage. The boardwalks are crowded with Christmas shoppers carrying bags of gifts wrapped in colorful paper and large satin bows. In the distance, church bells said it was noon. David carrying Sam, holding Hannah's hand, walked across the street to the eclectic Queen Anne and Victorian-style hotel, dressed in festive strings of lights, wreaths, and ornaments. Stairs lead to brickwork with painted window frames, Gabled roofs, and chimneys. David opened the door for Hannah and Sam. Wine-colored patterned carpets gave a cozy feeling to the large hotel lobby." Hannah noticed crystal chandeliers hanging from the ceiling like clusters of grapes.

"David," someday I will have a beautiful crystal chandelier in my home with electric lights." "You can have as many chandeliers as you want," he said.

David smiles at her, "Let's read the sign on the wall near the desk." "The Atlantic Café is open for breakfast, starting at 6 am, lunch, from eleven to two, closes at three, and opens again at five for dinner." "Hannah, this is what I like," said David pointing his finger at the list. "The Atlantic Room is a formal dining room. Dinner is served from five pm until eleven, Monday thru Thursday. Friday and Saturday night, there is dancing with live music until one am. Sunday morning brunch is served from seven am until three. Dinner is served from four pm until nine pm." "Hannah," do you like to dance?" asked David. "I love to dance," I don't know how, but I know that I will love it if you are my partner," said Hannah.

"No worries there," said David looking at her and kissing her cheek. Do you want lunch first or shop first?" asked David.

"I want to have lunch first. I think Sam is hungry, then shoes, then a toy."

"I love a woman that knows what she wants," said David squeezing her hand.

"David," before we go to the café," I want to take Sam over to the Christmas tree." I have never seen a tree with lights."

The tall, fragrant douglas fir tree was nestled in a corner by a winding white oak staircase leading to the upper floors. On the walls above the landing were paintings by famous artists. One of the pictures displayed a mythical figure, Sinterklaas, placing presents under the tree. Nearby was a group of carolers singing familiar Christmas songs.

" Let's go to the restaurant," said David. It looks busy, and I don't want to wait long for a table. I can smell steak. " After we are seated, I will take Sam to the bathroom and wash his hands."Sam, are your hands clean?" said Hannah. Sam looked at his hands and wiped them in his hair. Hands clean. now"

After lunch, the three walked to the children's clothing store several blocks away David kept a firm hold on Sam as they walked into the store. "I smell leather." Said, David. "Hannah, "What kind of shoes should we get," said David, looking at a brown high-top pair.

"I want them to be a good fit and sturdy," said Hannah, "I like the high top. They support his ankles." "If Sam's clothes or shoes didn't fit, he would throw them out the window," laughed Hannah. "Lilly and I didn't know how to be a mom."

After trying several pairs of shoes, Hannah and David agreed on the best fit for Sam.

While David paid for the shoes, Hannah put on Sam's new shoes and socks.

"I have waited a long time for this," said Hannah," tears running down her cheeks." So now it is on to the toy store. I can't imagine what toy he will want."

"I think Sam will lose or destroy these shoes in less than a week," said David. "I wouldn't want to bet on that one," said Hannah while walking out of the clothing store.

David and Hannah laughed at how Sam walked in his stiff new shoes. He kept looking at them and saying:" my new shoes."

David, Hannah, and Sam walked into the toy store. They met with odors of paint, leather, and new things.

"Sam," you can look around said, Hannah. The small boy was overwhelmed by what he saw. There were shelves of stuffed animals, dolls, books, and games. Sam went to the shelves of stuffed animals.

"Samie." Asked Hannah, you have many stuffed animals? Why don't you look at something else."

"NO!" said Sam while looking through the pile of stuffed animals. "I want a jiggity dog," said Sam looking at a little white dog. "I want this little dog too."

David laughed so hard that he had to step away from the scene. Hannah was blushing.

"Hannah," we better buy him one toy now and come back later." It is starting to snow, and the wind is blowing." I think I know what toy he will like," said David.

The three walked out of the store into swirls of snowflakes. Sam was cuddling his new stuffed toy, a black horse resembling Danny Boy.

"It's home again, Jiggidy Jig," said David laughing.

GETTING READY FOR THE CHRISTMAS PARTY

CHAPTER 9

"Thank you," auntie, for breakfast." You know my favorites are hotcakes, bacon, and eggs. I have a busy day ahead of me. " Freddie and Eral Gruen will help me at the livery stable, and we have to mend broken fences," said David.

"What happened to the fences?" asked Naomi, clearing the breakfast dishes.

"During the last snowstorm, a few feet of the fence fell. It is where our property joins the Gruen's," said David, putting on his winter coat and hat.

"I have a busy day, too," said Naomi putting dishes in the cupboard. The girls will be here t at 11:30 for lunch. My friends Loretta and Elaine will come over to help with the dresses and discuss how they wear their hair. After that, we will decorate Christmas cookies for the party next Saturday."

"I assume one of your ladies is Hannah," said David pulling on his gloves.

"You know that includes Hannah," said Naomi with a smile. Lilly, Sam, Gwen, Duff, Allison, and Junie are invited.."

"Please tell Hannah I don't know when I will be back here this afternoon," said David going out the back door. If I don't see Hannah tonight, I will see her tomorrow. The party is a week away. She doesn't know I am taking her to the Atlantic Room for dinner before the party," said David going out the back door.

Naomi watched David from the back door window. Today he was ridding Babe to get his chores done. Naomi watched David get into the saddle in one graceful leap. " That young man is so in Love. I don't think he knows what he is doing. " How I envy David and Hannah." Naomi thought about the husband she almost had. " Today is not a day for sad memories. It is Christmas, and there is much work and joy for all of us." Naomi wiped away tears while looking in the hall mirror. Some wrinkles were around her eyes and mouth. Perhaps someday, there would be a family for her to care for. "Maybe the family is already here?" thought Naomi.

"Hannah," hurry up," said Lilly impatiently. You look pretty enough for David. Let's get going!"

"I haven't seen David for two days, and I miss him," said Hannah while adjusting the ribbon in her hair.

"Don't forget, Lilly," we have to talk to Sister Catherine about a few things."

"Yes," said Lilly, "I hope she still has some information about us when we came here. "We have been in this place so long I can't remember what month or year Papa brought us."

"Lilly," I just thought of something," said Hannah putting on her coat. "Where is Sam?"

"Oh," no!" said Lilly. "We better look in the hallway before he gets too far away."

"There he is with Sister Catherine," said Hannah.

Sister Catherine and Sam were walking down the hallway toward their room. Sam got loose and ran to the girls.

"We have had a lovely conversation," said the smiling Nun. I knew you girls would be looking for Sam."

"We are sorry," said Hannah. "He gets away so fast."

"That's quite alright," said Sister Catherine. I am on my way to a meeting in Building B."

"We need to ask you one question," said Lilly, taking Sam's hand.

"What is it?" said Sister Catherine looking at her watch.

"We are wondering," said Hannah. If you can remember when papa brought us here?" We can't remember our old address or birthday."

"Miss Naomi and David said they would help us find pappa and maybe Mrs. Bruno." Said Hannah.

"We try to keep records on every child that comes here, and we record it when they leave, especially the adopted children," said Sister Catherine.

"Sister Agnus is looking at her watch again. "You girls have seen the shelves of record books in our office and downstairs. "It will take a while to find the information you want. "I can't start on it until after the Christmas Holidays," but I will put it on my essential list of things to do. You girls can help me."

"We would like that," said Lilly.

"I must hurry to the meeting, don't forget to remind me."

"I forgot to ask you girls, where are you off to? You will be beautifully dressed up."

"We are going to Miss Naomi's for lunch. Her friends are going to help fit our dresses." Said Hannah.

"And," said Lilly, we get to decorate Christmas cookies for the party next Saturday."

"That's right, and the party is next Saturday." "Sister Agnes and some other Sisters, myself included, will go for a little while.

It is a pleasure to see all of you girls and boys having fun. "I must hurry now. I won't forget to help you find your information." "I hope Gwen and Allison Junie are waiting for us," said Hannah.

The three walked down the stairs and into the front hall.

"We have been waiting for you," said Gwen. "We don't want to keep Miss Naomi waiting."

The girls chattered about their new dresses, hair, and the party at Miss Naomi's.

Duff rang the buzzer at the door. They could hear the footsteps of someone coming to open it.

"Welcome, girls and little boys," said a smiling Naomi. We are so glad you are here Please come in. "I want you girls to meet two good friends, "Elaine" and Loretta." "They will help with your dresses, hair, and cookie decorations.

"We will eat lunch first, here in the kitchen." Elaine and Loretta brought food to go with what I have prepared," said Naomi, putting some platters 0f food in the oven above the stove. Take a plate from the drainboard, scoop up anything you want, and sit at the table. I think I have enough chairs."

"When you finish with lunch," said Miss Naomi, I want all of you to scrap and rinse your plate and glass, then pile the dishes in the sink" We will wash them later. "After lunch, we will get started on your dress and hair," said Naomi. The little boys can play with Miss Kitty and the basket of toys I have for them. We have some trousers and vests for the boys to try on."

"Thank you, Fred, for helping me repair the fence," said David stepping back to look at their work. I hope they patched the hole in the barbed wire and will stay until spring; then, I need to replace several feet of fence."

"David, where do you want me to go next?" asked Fred. "Please go to the livery stable until the horses get groomed and the stalls cleaned. Then you can go home. It has been a long day for both of us. "I still have to check on a colt for Dr. Wade.

The horse stepped into some wire. I need to rub on some medicine and change the bandage, then I'll get home and see my family," said David.

"Are you going to work for Dr. Wade full-time after you graduate from veterinary school?" asked Fred while picking up tools.

"I hope to for a while, then start my practice closer to home." I still have to work in the livery stable." "Maybe you can think about working full-time at the stable," said David, checking Babe's saddle. I have to work all I can. I am taking on new responsibilities, and I want to be ready. I will have electricity put in the big farmhouse and indoor plumbing. Auntie says it costs a lot of money. She has some voltage but not the whole house."

"I think you will ask Hannah to marry you," said Fred with a grin."

*Does it show that much?" said David as he rode on Babe. "*yes!* I am happy for you, said Fred.

The afternoon went by quickly—Miss Naomi's sewing room filled with the sweet spirit of girlhood trying on a first-time party dress. The young ladies reminded Naomi of graceful ballerinas pirouetting with swirling silk and satin garments, accented in pale lavender colors, blushing pink, wintergreen, and Christmas red gliding like bouquets of Silhouettes in the thin winter sun.

Loretta and Elaine said their goodbyes and told the girls they were looking forward to helping them prepare for the party next Saturday.

"I have an idea," said Naomi wiping a wisp of hair from her eye. "Since we still have more food, why don't all stay for dinner?" We will eat at about 6: o.' clock. David should be here by that time. Let's wash the lunch dishes and set the table in the dining room. I will get a tablecloth and napkins. As you dry the plates, put them on the table. There will be nine of us. I will show you where I want everyone to sit," Naomi unfolded a large tablecloth.

"I am the lady of the house, so I will sit at the head of the table. David is the man of the house; he will sit at the other end of the table. Sam, Hannah, Allison, and Junie will be on his right. On the left of David are Lilly, Duff, and Gwen. Two tall tapers will be our centerpiece."

Naomi enjoyed the evening. She loved listening to laughter and chatter from the Girls. Sam and Duff were playing with their toys. They loved to watch Miss Kitty chase her ball.

"I think I hear Ring barking," said Naomi running to the back porch window. David always brings his dog with him. "David and Ring are here," said Naomi opening the back door. Ring pushed into the house, ran to the kitchen, and shook the snow from his coat. Naomi gave him a bone. The dog went into the living room, lay down by the warm fire in the fireplace, and enjoyed his treat. Hearing David's voice, Sam dropped his toy and ran to the back door saying, "Davidid." The little boy ran full steam into David's waiting arms. David barely closed the door when Hannah flung her arms around David's waist and put her head on his shoulder behind Sam.

"With a big smile and the sound of emotion, David said, this is the kind of homecoming I have been waiting for."

David sat on a bench to take off his boots. Sam was already on his lap. Shy little Duff wanted to sit on David's lap, also. Sam pushed him away and said, "no," my Davdid" Duff backed away and looked at David. David felt compassion for the lonely child with a lump in his throat. Duff's blond hair almost covered his brown eyes. His narrow nose matched his thin lips. The little boy had both hands folded and held high on his chest. When David invited him to sit on his lap, Duff looked at Sam to ensure it was okay. Again Sam pushed Duff away, saying, "NO!" my Davidid!" David pulled the frail-looking little boy onto his lap. He hugged Duff and kissed him on top of his head.

"Sam," there is room for both of you boys to sit on my lap." Sam looked at Duff, sitting quietly, then looked up at David. "okay," David, he can stay."

"That's my good boy," said David. He cuddled both little boys and then asked them if they would like to help him remove his boots.

Both little boys said "yes," and soon laughed and played.

"It is time to come to the table. Dinner is ready," announced Lilly

Naomi instructed the girls where she wanted the bowls of food placed on the table and reminded them of her seating chart. Everyone sat in their appointed place. "David," will you say "Grace?" said Naomi

"Yes," said David. "Everyone, please join hands."

David recited the blessing that he had remembered from childhood.

"Thank you, Father, for this family and keeping us safe. Bless the food for the good of our bodies, and bless the hands that prepared it. Amen." Everyone said, *"AMEN."*

"David, you start dishing up each plate, and I will help pass it around, said Naomi.

David kept watching his auntie smile and have fun. She waited on the girls, ensured they had everything, and laughed with them. Naomi watched David smile and laugh. He loved that Hannah Duff Sam was near him.

David saw Ring and Miss Kitty wander into the dining room and hide under the table. Naomi said, "don't feed the animals at the table."

David quietly gave Ring a large piece of meat, and Miss Kitty got a treat, also. The dog and cat stayed under the table, waiting for another crumb. They didn't have to wait long. There was a lot of food under Sam's chair. Hannah couldn't stop giggling.
Miss Naomi saw the pets but had too much fun to say anything.

Dinner was over, apple pie and oatmeal cookies, then it was time to wash the dishes. David and Hannah offered to clean them, but Naomi said, why don't you sit in front of the fireplace with Hannah?"

"I can't turn that down," said David taking Hannah's hand.
Everyone in the kitchen kept peeking to hear what the young couple said.

David and Hannah talked in a low voice. Sometimes they laughed, and sometimes David stole a kiss.

The clock in the hallway said it was 8 o'clock. "It is time for you girls and boys to go home and get ready for bed," said Naomi. It has been a long, fun day for all of us."

"Are we going to take our dresses with us tonight?" asked Junie.

"No," said Naomi, I will keep them here because you don't have space in your room." Some of them have to be pressed or stitched.." I will get them to you Friday afternoon or Saturday morning. A carriage will pick you up for the party at about 5:30 Saturday afternoon at your home."

"Everyone put on your coat, scarf, mittens, and boots. David will walk you home," said Naomi looking at David."

David nodded and helped Sam and Duff put on their coat and boots.

"David," please come in the kitchen for a minute," said Naomi softly.

"What is it, auntie?" said David walking into the kitchen.

"I made you some sandwiches, wrapped up some cake and cookies, and a meat bone for Ring.

When you are getting thin from working hard and not eating enough, Naomi said to have a sandwich when you return from walking the girls home. I will put your sandwiches in the icebox."

Everyone said their "goodbyes" and started their walk in the crunchy snow.

They were walking hand in hand. David and Hannah enjoyed watching the girls make snowballs. Sam and Duff threw the snowballs.

"I love walking in the snow on a winter night," said Hannah, laying her head on David's arm.

"Me too," said David pulling Hannah closer to him.

In the distance, the couple could see the sign that said "City of New York Children's Orphanage.

"I wish the sign could say *home* instead of "*orphanage,*" said Hannah. Lilly and I have been here so long. It feels like home." "I am so lucky to have you and Miss Naomi," said Hannah.

"Auntie" is the only mother I remember," said David. "She takes good care of me, and l look after her."

Hannah opened the door to soft lamplight and a cozy fire on the stove. Most of the children had gone to bed. Sister Catherine was sitting at the guest table in the corner of the room. She looked up from her book and said goodnight to each child as they came in.

"Lilly." Will you please take Sam and get him ready for bed?" asked Hannah. "I want to visit with David for a few more minutes."

"Okay," said Lilly, I know why you want to stay out here; it's so you can kiss."

"That's right," said David, "thank you for looking after Sam." "Hannah, let's sit on the bench under that tree in the yard." "I am ready to rest," said Hannah, " think you have something on your mind."

"You are always on my mind." Said David while walking to the bench. "Hannah," I want to take you someplace special to both of us," said David taking Hannah's hand. I don't know the exact time yet," but I want to take you to dinner before the Christmas party."

"Where," said Hannah, gazing into David's eyes.

"I want to take you to the Atlantic Room for dinner and dancing next Saturday. "Will you go with me?" "We will go for about two hours before the party starts." The party is in one of the ballrooms on the main floor, and the restaurant is upstairs near a beautiful veranda."

I can hardly wait said Hannah squeezing David's hand. "I will wear a new dress, go to a fancy restaurant and party, and be with you." Said Hannah. "I am so happy."

"I am happy too," said David kissing Hannah on her cheek.

It's getting colder out here," said David walking Hannah to the front porch. I better get you inside the house."

"Would you like to go to six o'clock mass with me in the morning?" or at eight am.? I want the eight am mass. I will have more time to get ready replied Hannah.

I" will come over about seven am.," said David. After church, we will go for a sleigh ride if there is enough snow. David kissed Hannah goodbye, holding her tight in his arms. "Someday, we won't have to say goodbye on a front porch; it will be in our home." thought David. Hannah quietly opened the door and tiptoed across the room.

"Is that you, Hannah?" said Sister Catherine. "Yes," said Hannah, I hope I didn't disturb you."

"No!" said the Sister, closing her book. "Come over here and sit down. I want to talk to you about something."

Hannah took off her coat, scarf, and mittens and hung them on the coat rack.

"Would you like to have tea?" asked Sister Catherine.

"Yes," said Hannah sitting down at the table. Hannah loves Sister Catherine. She is not only a wise counselor but also a friend. "I want to talk to you about David." "You like him, don't you?"

said Sister Catherine, pouring tea.

"Yes," said Hannah. I have never felt this way about a boy. There is something magical about David; he is kind, wise, and generous.

"Do you think he has feelings for you?" asked the Sister.

"I am sure he has feelings for me." "He takes me places. We will have dinner in the Atlantic dining room before the party."

"Yes," said Hannah. We get along nicely. David loves Sam as much as Lilly and I do." He likes to kiss me too," Hannah blushed, trying not to look at Sister Catherine. Hannah felt the warm, gentle touch of Sister Catherine's hands, reminding her of mama's soft hands. The Sister saw a brief reflection of herself as a young girl. She remembered running from Love; now, there was no turning back. She is married to God and the Church.

"Sister," said Hannah leaning on her elbows, how do I know that David loves me, and I love him?"

"That is one of the mystical and spiritual parts of love," said the smiling Sister. Again taking Hannah's hands in hers, she continued, Love is a gift of the spirit, and we become immersed in it. Love is the crowning glory of The Good Shepherd. Love cannot exist without Wisdom."Wisdom is the loving instructor, teaching you how to live and love." Hannah," you already know David loves you, and you love him. Pray about it and have confidence in yourself and D.avid. Most of all, have faith in God."

Hannah said goodnight to Sister Catherine and went upstairs to her room. Lilly was sleeping peacefully in her bed. Sam was asleep on a crib mattress on the floor between the two beds. He outgrew his crib and still didn't have his bed. Hannah went to the window and looked out at the night sky. She always thought the blinking stars were her loved ones looking after her and Lilly. The city looked friendly; now, there was electric light. It was hard to understand that pulling a chain or turning on a switch made light, but I am glad we have it. "Maybe someday I will live in a house filled with light," thought Hannah."

Capricorn ushered in winter solutes with a glimmering blanket of snow. Naked trees dressed in their fresh white coat, evergreen trees displayed heaps of snowflakes on their outstretched branches.

On the twenty-first of December, the Saturday before Christmas, the day of the Christmas party finally arrived. At one o'clock, Miss Naomi, Loretta, and Elain came to the orphanage with piles of dazzling silken and satin dresses accented with lace and bows. Sister Agnes permitted the girls to change in the dining hall after lunch. They promised they would put the tables back in place before supper. Hannah was first to get dressed, and Naomi coifed her hair. Loretta and Elaine's expertise.was extended to the other girls. David is going to pick her up at three o'clock. He wants to take her around the city to see Christmas lights displayed in the big department stores. He made a reservation for six in the Atlantic Side dining room. They are opening an hour early until Christmas to accommodate the hotel guests. David plans for surprises and romance for the young woman to accept his marriage proposal.

Lilly and Gwen watched Davi's carriage arrive at 3O'clock. He was not driving. The driver jumped down and opened the door. Handsome. David stepped down, wearing a black tuxedo and bow tie topped with a black wool overcoat. He was carrying a little box trimmed in pink satin ribbon. He hurried to the front door. A scramble of young girls announced at the bottom of the stairs, " David is here carrying a gift."When David came in, Lilly said Hannah was upstairs. Miss Naomi is Still combing Hannahs's hair.

"Thanks, Willy said David, patting Lilly on top of her. Head. "your moment, said Naomi to Hannah. Go to David and let him see you walk down the stairs."

Black lace appliques on the elbow-length sleeves and hemline gracefully descended the stairs to David looking at her. She began to tremble when he extended his hand and led her to his waiting arms. "Hannah," you are beautiful! Thank you, David," said Hannah, "I feel beautiful."

David placed the small box in Hannah's shaky hands. "Open it," said David. It is for you." Everyone watched as Hannah opened the box and said," miniature roses in my favorite colors of pink and red." What do I do with them?" Naomi stepped in and said, "I will pin this corsage on your dress." your prince is waiting."

Won't you come to my garden? My roses want to see you, Richard Sheridan

THE CHRISTMAS PARTY

CHAPTER 10

David helped Hannah put on her coat and wrapped her shawl around her shoulders.

"It is freezing outside, and the walkways may be slippery," said David opening the door to winter fury.

The couple walked with caution to their waiting carriage. Mr. Gruen jumped off the driver's platform of the carriage, tipped his hat to Hannah, and opened the carriage door.

"I put several woolen blankets on the seat for the two of you," said Fred

"I will turn on a side street near the hotel. There is an awning-covered entrance for carriages. "I will take you there and come back at midnight."

"Don't worry," said David. We can enjoy the warmth of the hotel."

"One more thing," said Fred, "did you notice that Danny Boy is wearing his Christmas red coat, and there are jingle bells tied to the carriage door handles.?"

Fred opened the door a little more. Hannah and David laughed when they looked at the frosted windows of the orphanage. A small nose is pressed against the glass. David smiled when he saw a pint-size boy pointing his finger and making a noise.

"The children will be t happy that Gwen, Allison, and June will stay with them and put them to bed.

Hannah tried to scrape the frosted window of the carriage with her gloved hand. A little cracked ice gave the glass its holiday design.

"David, I see the snow on the trees. I love winter. It is a coloscope wonderland."

"When we get closer to the city, we should see the glow of electric light," remarked David.

"I just thought of something," said Hannah. I am glad Danny is wearing a winter coat. What about his feet? Won't they get cold?"

"Don't worry, said David with a grin; he has his winter shoes on."

Hannah thought a few seconds, then said, "David, you are a tease!"

The couple relaxed for a few moments reflecting on the evening's magic and exchanging memories of long ago. The rhythmic sway of the carriage and Danny Boy will always be in their hearts. Hannah recalled the lonely nights in the orphanage and her lack of trust in adults. Papa left them at the orphanage after Mama died. He never came back like he said he would. All Hannah and Lilly had were each other and a dark, unfriendly place to call home.

David thought about Christmas past and opening presents with no one but Naomi. She was all his family except fraternal grandfather Martin living in a nursing home. He is too frail for the long ride to Aunties. After Christmas, Grandfather loved it when his handsome little grandson David came to visit and would read to him and tell him about all the animals he would care for. Auntie always had a delicious holiday dinner for friends and children from the nearby orphanage.

Things will be different from now on, thought David. God answered my prayer and put Hannah in my life. God gives abundantly. Sam would be in his life too. He knows Hannah will never give up on Sam. How could he not love Sam" His family would grow. The new year would bring him a wife and son.

Fred guided Danny Boy to the carriage entrance of the hotel. A doorman dressed in holiday colors opened the carriage door for the couple. They walked a short distance to a heavy door that led to

Small entry hall. French doors opened to the main lobby and the sweet scents of the season.

"David," do you mind if I walk to the tree and look at its beautiful decorations.?"

No," said David. I must go to the reception desk and check our dinner reservations." He put his hand on hers and said, "This special evening is for us." Hannah looked at him like he had a secret or a surprise.

The Douglas fir tree is standing at attention near the fireplace, with green, blue, and red electric lights looking like elves racing on tiny sleds around the tree. Ribbons tied on the branches and colorful ornaments add to the festivity. Flames from the fireplace moved like ballerinas dancing and leaping on top of a music box. *I wish Mama and papa could enjoy this*, thought Hannah.

She watched David as he approached the reception desk. The blacktails of his overcoat swayed in the breeze. As he walked, He turned around and smiled at her. Hannah could see David at the reception desk, talking to the clerk. She watched him shake his

head yes, sign a paper, and put it in his jacket's breast pocket. He was ready to walk to Hannah when he heard a female voice say,

"David," David Kilmore, I have been looking for you! "

Nary BethJordan was walking toward him. Her long blond curls bounced on the shoulders of her low-cut dress, revealing an ample bosom that bobbed like dumplings in the stew. Before David could speak, she threw her arms around him and kissed his cheek. David looked past Mary and smiled at Hannah, shrugging his shoulders. Hannah enjoyed the spot David was in. Mary kept hugging and kissing him. Finally, David gently pushed her away.

"What do you want, Mary Beth?"

I am here with my grandparents and parents. We have reservations in the Atlantic Room. So you can sit with us, and I want the first dance with you, the last dance, and as many as I can. We will continue school in January and graduate in June.

My nursing campus is near your campus. So we can go to a lot of parties together."

David looked at Hannah and motioned her to come to him. "Mary Beth Hanah is my date. She will get all the dances". "There are always the tag dances, " snapped Mary Beth, " I will get some of them. You don't want me to embarrass you, David?"

Mary looked at Hannah with jealousy while Hannah walked to David.

Are you that orphan from near here?" Are you that orphaned girl from the nearby orphanage?"

"That's me," said Hannah with a smile.

"This must be a big event for you, going out to dinner and wearing a used dress. You don't mind if I dance with David, do you?"

"No," said Hannah, I don't mind, but David might not go for it."

David pulled Hannah closer, kissed her cheek, and said to

Betsy. "Hannah is the only one for me, and this is a special night for us. We want to have a quiet dinner together and dance to midnight."

Mary Beth felt anger and rage toward Hannah as the couple walked up the stairs to the dining room. David put his arm around Hannah. They were talking and laughing. She walked toward the stairs to see if she could see where they were going to sit. They stopped at the cloakroom. David carefully helped Hannah remove her coat, then wrapped her shawl around her shoulders. David hung his overcoat next to Hanna's in the closet. Then, hand in hand, they walked to the hostess's desk and got their table number. They were seated at table five, dressed with sparkling glasses and fine china. David pulled out Hannah's chair. She smiled.

Hannah felt like a beautiful princess sitting across the table from David.

"David, I love where we are sitting. The fireplace is near, and the glassed-in Terrace Room is across from us."

"I like it, too," said David. We are close to the orchestra. They should be playing soon."

David reached over and took Hannah's hands in his. There is something important I want to talk to you about." The waiter interrupted them, asking, "May I bring you something to drink, a cocktail, champagne, coffee, or tea?"

"Hannah, would you like to try some hot apple cider? I will have some. wine. I think you will like the cider."

Again David tenderly held Hannah's hands and began to say what was on his mind.

"Our drinks are here," said Hannah. She took a sip and said, "This reminds me of apple pie."

"Hannah, I want to ask you something. Will you marry me?"

Hannah choked, nearly spilling her cider, and said, "You want to marry me?"

"Yes," said David. "I have been thinking about it for a long time. But, the first day I saw you, I knew you were the one for me."

"David," said Hannah, "I don't have anything to give you. I still have one more year of high school. I have never been to a wedding. I wouldn't know where to start. What about Sam and Lilly? I can't leave them. I want to marry you more than anything in this world. What you see is what you get."

"I am willing to take a chance on you if you are willing to take a chance on me," said David.

He reached into his breast pocket and took out a dark blue velvet box. He opened it and said, "Hannah, this ring is for you. Hannah put her hands on her face and blushed. It is beautiful. I love the solitaire diamond. You didn't need to spend so much money on me. I will be happy with anything you choose for me." Yes, I will marry you."

"Let me put it on your finger," said David. Hold out your left hand." He slipped the ring on her tiny finger. " I think you will like this family heirloom. My grandmother Martin and my mother wore this ring at their weddings. They told auntie that whoever got married first could choose the engagement ring or the wedding band. So I chose the engagement ring to buy. I want to buy you a wedding ring. I hope we can pass it down to our children. Next week I will take you to a jewelry store to have it cleaned and sized."

"Does anyone know about our engagement except you and me?" said Hannah while admiring her ring.

"Yes," said David. I had to tell Auntie. She kept the rings in a locked jewelry box. She is so happy and wants to help us in any way, especially at the wedding. I have one thing to say about Auntie. I love her very much. She can get pushy and want to do things her way. This wedding is for you and me. Don't be afraid to speak up if you want to do something different."

"I will never do or say anything to upset her," said Hannah, still admiring her ring.

"Good evening, sir and ma'am. May I get you something to drink? Or perhaps champagne, coffee, or tea?"

"Yes," said David. " I would like two seafood appetizers and everything that comes with it. The best in the house! Tonight is a special evening for us. It sounds like the orchestra is ready to play. David pulled Hannah's chair out and said to the waiter, " We will order after this dance ."

"May I have this dance, Mrs. Kilmore?"

"Yes," said Hannah, "I would love to dance with you."

"They are playing one of my favorite love songs," said David. "I will always remember this night and the music of " Clair de Lune." This is the first time we danced as an engaged couple, "By the Light of the Moon," said David.

Hannah lay her head on David's chest. David guided her around the Terrace Room dance floor in swirls of silk, diamonds, and l accents of love in grace and charm. Hannah looked up at David and smiled. He looked down at the lovely woman in his arms. Before she knew it, David, with his hands on her waist, picked her up and twirled her like a ballerina on a music box. The new moon cast her silken beams on the young couple while they kissed in tireless passion and love.

The orchestra conductor announced they were going to take a twenty-minute break. David and Hannah walked back to the candlelight table to the sound of applause.

"Are they clapping for us?" said Hannah.

"I think they are applauding your beauty," said David.

"I think it is for both of us," said Hannah blushing at the attention.

When they got to their table, there were menus on their plates. "From the looks of these menus, dinner will be expensive,"

said Hannah trying to read French.

"Hannah," said David," please let me worry about the expenses."

I know how to save money and have waited a long time for this evening."

"Me too," said Hannah, still looking at the menu.

"The only language I know is English, so I am not much help. We can ask the server about it. I only know medical words like jiggidy jig." laughed David.

Hanna hid her blushing face behind her hand with a diamond on her finger.

"Hannah, would you like me to order for you?' said David, turning the menu pages.

"It depends on what you want to order," said Hannah trying not to blush.

"I have too much love and respect to tell you what to do," said David. "You can order me to do anything. You can chase me, and I will let you catch me," teased David.

"You are a tease like me; one more reason I love you," said Hannah.

"What time is it."

"It is almost seven-fifteen," said David, looking at his watch. "The children should be coming at any time. For the Christmas party."

"Let's go down to the first landing," said Hannah, admiring her beautiful engagement ring.

"I hear a lot of noise. I think some of them are from the children that spied on us while we got into the carriage," said David.

HANNAH

The lobby doors opened. A group of young children came in to have fun playing games and open Christmas presents.

"Hannah, I see Sam. He is looking up here, trying to find us." "Now he is jumping up and down and throwing a fit," laughed Hannah.

The couple stood on the stair landing, smiling and proud of the little boy named Sam, that was hollering and had wiped his sticky hands in his hair,

"David said to Hannah," Sam looked up at us. He is trying to say I am down here."

"Just think, Hannah, he will be all ours, and we will enjoy every precious minute of him."

"The children will have their dinner, then dessert and presents," said David. Let's dance a few more dances before we go down there."

"I hope Lilly has to clean him up. But, unfortunately, the party hasn't started yet, and he probably needs a warm cloth to wash his hands and hair," laughed David.

Hannah put her tiny hand into his large hand as they walked up the stairs

M maybe we can include Duff in our family thought, David. He remembered mama saying two toddlers are less work than one. They have each other to play with, someone who understands toddler talk. If Hannah says yes about Duff, I will be a hands-on papa. I want children of our own. I will be a good papa, no matter how many we have.

"We will know everything Sam ate." It will start from his hair down to his shirt and shoes." said David.

Hannah thought about how much fun it would be to include Duff in the family. Sam and Duff get along so well. I worry about Duff. He is so frail and pale. Sam would see that kids didn't pick on Duff even though he is two years older than Sam." Hannah's thoughts were interrupted by a familiar tonne of voice.

"When David and Hannah got to the bottom of the stairs, they heard Betsy angrily calling "Hannah.!"

" I will take care of this for you," said David

No one talks to you like that," said David, feeling his temper starting to get hot.

"Don't worry about me. I can deal with Betsy myself," said Hannah. However," Don't go too far away if something goes wrong." David put his arm around Hannah's shoulders and pulled her close. If Betsy thinks she can take me down, she's going down too." said Hannah.

"David was nervous. He has never seen this side of Hanna, Mary Beth." I didn't notice you were here," said Hannah trying not to laugh.

"I want you to know David loves me!" said Mary Beth, shaking her finger at Hannah

"On what evidence do you base that assumption?!" Hannah shot back.

"Well," said Betsy, ready to pounce on Hannah with the fangs of a snake.

"We have known each other since we were three years old. David has kissed me many times. He wanted to go further, but I said no. I will save myself for our wedding night."

"You aren't from here. "No one knows where you came from. I am studying to be a nurse. You could never get a high-paying job like that. David is studying the care of pigs, chickens, and goats." Hannah was having fun with Betsy. She told Betsey you would know who to call when you got sick! Don't forget, Miss Betsy, who has the engagement ring?" You say I don't know where I am from. The essential things are that I understand where I am going. We are on our way to our engagement party. We will send you an invitation to our wedding."

"Hannah," let s go to the entry hall. I want to talk to you," said David

"Oh no," thought Hannah. I have upset him." The night of our engagement. I am not going to let a stuck-up girl like Betsy run me down or tell me what to do," thought Hannah.

"I hope I haven't upset David." That is the last thing I want to do to the man I will marry."

"Hannah said; I am sorry," David."

"I am sorry, too," said David.

" I don't like what she said about you being an animal doctor." "You put her in her place with style and grit. Maybe I won't let you catch me when you chase me. You are fierce," teased David. "Don't worry, David. I will chase you and catch you. Then I will beat your butt with a broom."

"I wish we were getting married tonight," said David

"I feel that way also. I will have three men to look after. I have to be fierce."

David pulled Hannah into his arms and gently kissed her lips. "We better go see what Sam is into," said David.

Have you noticed Duff laughs at everything Sam does or says?" said Hannah

"Yes," said David looking at Hannah,

Hand in Hand, David and Hannah walked across the hotel lobby and went into the "party room."

"It is noisy in here," said Hanna

"I feel Sam will find us before we find him," said David like a proud father.

"If we find Duff first, Sam is nearby." Said Hannah.

David felt a tug on his jacket. A tiny boy with jam in his hair and a new shirt in his hand looked up. Next to him was Duff with a shirt in his hand.

What have you got there," said David kneeling to see the shirts.

"I opened a box, and there was a new 'shit" in it " Can I wear it now."?

"Yes," said Hannah, I will help you. I can't believe what I heard him say, looking at David.

"I wanted a toy." Said Sam. When he smiled, Hannah and David could see what he had for dinner and dessert.

"San, how did you get jam in your hair?" asked David.

I ran into some jam," said Sam while looking at his new shirt. "That's a good answer," Hannah giggled.

Duff patted David on his shoulder and said: " see, I got a new" cert" while holding it to his chest.

Hannah and David couldn't keep from laughing.'

THE ENGAGEMENT

CHAPTER 11

"Soon, we will know what Sam ate by looking at his clothes," laughed David.

"All we have to do is get the jam out of his hair, wipe the crumbs from his chin, and he probably has wet drawers." Said Hannah laughing.

Hannah was thinking about Duff. "He will be as clean now as when he got here "Sometimes I worry about Duff," said David. He looks frail and does not have much energy. There are dark circles under Duff's eyes. What do you think about adopting Duff along with Sam?"

"The boys are best friends," said Hannah. I don't think it would be wise to separate them. They could share the same bedroom for a while."

When David and Hannah reached the bottom of the stairs, they heard a female voice shouting,

"Hannah! I want to talk to you!"

"That has to be Betsy," said David with concern. I wonder what she wants?" "Hey, Hannah!" I want to talk to you. David wants me rather than you.'

David felt anger toward Betsy. I will take care of her. She has no right to yell at you."

"Please don't," I want to talk to her," said Hannah putting her hand on David's arm.

HANNAH

David put his arm around Hannah's shoulders and pulled her closer.

"If Betsy thinks she can take me down, she is going down too," thought Hannah with a mischievous smile.

David was nervous. He had never seen the aggressive side of Hannah.

"Hi, Mary Beth," said Hannah, I just noticed you standing here."

"I want you to know that David is in love with me, said Mary Beth. "We sneak off to secret places. And we have known each other since we were about three years old. David loves to kiss me and has wanted to go further. I told him I was saving myself for our wedding night."

"You will have to save for a long time," laughed Hannah. "You aren't from here," said Mary Beth. You speak with a

funny accent.

"I think you have an accent," said Hannah smugly.

"I am going to school to be a nurse. I will earn a lot of money and take care of sick people. You could never do anything like that. David is learning to take care of chickens, pigs, and goats." "You will know who to call when you get sick," said Hannah.

Don't forget; I am the one wearing a diamond engagement ring. So I not only know where I came from, I know where I am going. David and I are celebrating our engagement. I' will make sure you get a wedding invitation."

"Come on, Hannah," said David. We better get the kids". You know how to take care of yourself."

"I didn't like it when she made fun of animal doctors," said Hannah.

You told her off pretty well," David teased. Maybe I shouldn't let you catch me; you are fierce," said David.

"I not only can catch you, but I will also beat your butt with a broom." laughed Hannah. I have to take care of three men, so I have to be fast," warned Hannah with a smile.

David pulled Hannah into his arms and sweetly kissed her rosy pink lips." I wish we could be married tonight, though, David."

"We better find the boys and see what Sam is into. I hope Lilly brought enough clean clothes. Have you noticed Duff laughs at everything Sam does?" Said, David.

"Why not? Said Hannah," We laugh too."

Hand in hand, the young couple walked across the hotel lobby towards the party room. Of course, they could hear children playing, running, and childhood noise. But, like any proud parent, they knew one noisy one was Sam, and the laughing one was Duff.

David opened the door for Hannah to the party room. The children are like a flock of lambs "The good shepherds" have to run fast to keep up with them."

David felt a tug on his long coat. "I am right here said a pint-size adorable sticky lamb looking up at him.

David knelt to hear what Sam was trying to say to him. "What have you got there?" said David.

"This is my new "shit." Said Sam. It is clean."

Hannah was trying not to laugh. "I can't believe what he just said."

"I wanted a toy, not something to wear."

"It is a lovely shirt," said Hannah. I will help you put it on.
"I think we will be able to find out what he had for dinner," David examined Sam's clothing.
"Why is your hair so sticky?" asked David.
"I ran into some jam," said Sam, still looking at the shirt he wished was a toy.
David felt some little arms around his neck and a small head resting on the back of his shoulder. "Is that you, Duff? Said, David
"Yes." Said the small boy.
David picked up both boys and stood so he could talk to them. Sam was kissing his face, and Duff waved his new shirt for all to see.

"Is that a new shirt?" said Hannah stroking his hair. "Yes," said Duff, it's a:" cert' not a toy David and Hannah laughed and played with their soon-to-be little sons.

Hannah wrapped her arms around her future husband and precious children.

"Have you kids scene seen Lilly or Gwen?" asked David. "Yes," said Duff, they keep talking to boys."

"Hi, Hannah and David," said Lilly. The boys are having a great time." They only got upset when they opened a gift, which was clothes instead of toys.

"The girls wanted dolls. Sometimes they liked clothes or hair ribbons." So said Sam, still trying to unbutton his new shirt.

"David, I want down," said Sam. David gently set the two boys down on the floor.

Before anyone could stop Sam, he ran over to the punch table and stood on his tiptoes to get himself a cup of "red stuff," also known as juice or punch. His little fingers couldn't grasp the cup. A stream of fresh, red stuff zig-zagged down his shirt and sweater and finally landed on his shoes.

"Sam, let me help you," said Lilly rushing to the scene and cleaning up Sam again.

"I am sorry said Lilly, wiping off her hands with a cloth and mopping up the floor.

"Okay," Hanna, banana nose, show us your beautiful engagement ring," replied Lilly.

"How do you know about my new ring?" questioned Hannah. "Miss Naomi is so happy she couldn't keep quiet any longer.

"Said Lilly.

"Yes," David and I are engaged," Hannah held out her left hand so everyone could see the sparkling .ring. Gwen, Junie, Allison, and Lilly were excited about the engagement and being near David.

"Welcome to the family," said Lilly. I always wanted an older brother so I could meet his friends and wear his shirts and sweaters."

"I always wanted a little sister named "Willy. Now I have both a beautiful woman and someone to tease." Said David looking at Hannah.

"It is ten-thirty," said David looking at his watch. Sam and duff should be in bed,"

"I know what you and Hannah want to do said Lilly, trying to embarrass her sister. You want to kiss. She made smacking sounds, which did cause Hannah to blush.

"That sounds like a good thing to do," said David hugging Hannah.

"Go find Auntie Naomi and tell her all of you are ready to go home. I think Duff is almost asleep," said David. Tomorrow is Christmas Day. The boys will have another fun day opening presents.

"Come here." let's go upstairs and dance the night away, my sweet blushing rose."

Everyone watched with envy the betrothed, hand in hand, walk across the lobby and go upstairs to dance to the melodies of love and moonlight. David cradled Hannah in his arms and hoped the orchestra would continue to play for several more Hours. They looked at each other in love, romance, and passion as David twirled her in swirls of satin and silk accented by The light of the moon.

On Christmas Day, Scorpio sprinted across the Eastern Seaboard, leaving imprints of snow gardens with accents of heaps of flakes clinging to naked tree branches while icy mud puddles gleamed in the thin winter sun.

"For thy love is better than wine," Song of Solomon 1-3

TO GRANDFATHER R'S HOUSE, WE GO

CHAPTER 12

Miss Naomi and David decided it would be fun to take the children on a sleigh ride and visit Grandfather Kilmore in the city the day after Christmas. Naomi piled the sled and carriage with presents, candy, cookies, and a picnic basket for her grandfather and friends. His delight will be meeting Sam, Duff, Lilly, and Hannah. David and Hannah hoped he would agree to walk her down the aisle at their wedding. Fred Gruen offered to drive the sled, pulled by Babe, and David and Hannah would ride in the carriage with Danny-Boy in the harness. David and Hannah wanted to spend as much time alone as possible. Soon David would be returning to veterinary school. They would see each other only on weekends.

"Hannah," David, and Miss Naomi are here," said Lilly while buttoning her coat. They brought a sled and a carriage."

Sam heard David was there and ran out the door in his stocking feet. "Davidid" Davdid." Said the little boy. He was quickly retrieved and brought back indoors. Hannah put his shoes, boots, coat, and scarf on him. David knelt so Sam could crash into his waiting arms.

"Duff," you come too." Said David holding out his arms to receive the boys.

David lifted the boys into the sled. Driven by Fred, He helped Hannah onto the carriage seat to snuggle next to each other.

"Driving to the city is becoming familiar," said Hannah while resting her head on David's arm. I am sure Danny Boy knows the way. He also likes to go through mud puddles."

"Hannah," would you like to dance on New Year's Eve at the Atlantic side Hotel?" Then, we will have dinner, spend the rest of the evening in each other's arms, and start the New Year together." "David," you are romantic," said Hannah, kissing him. Will we see each other at the weekend?"

"I," think I could come home every other weekend, and you could spend the following weekend with me. There is a dormitory where you can stay. Unfortunately, you can't stay in my dorm." I will go home for spring break. As graduation gets closer, I may have to remain in school, especially for finals."

"David," tell me more about grandfather Kilmore," said Hannah w, snuggling up close to David, signaling Danny Boy to go a little faster. I wish I could tell Danny to go around mud puddles." laughed David. I think Danny has been on this route so many times he falls asleep While walking, he is a good horse, and I hope we have him for a long time. I will tell you all about my grandfather, but I want you to meet him first."

"Are we almost there?" said Hannah teasing.

"Yes, Hannah, we are almost there. Grandfather's home is a few blocks east of the Atlantic Side hotel. I think he is happy there. He doesn't have to worry about meals and has friends playing cards with him. He loves company and family. "

The carriage made a right turn to the top of a hill.

"See that large building at the bottom of the hill," said David; that is where he has lived for about eight years."

"I see a sign posted on the lawn. What does it say?" asked Hannah.

"It says Pennington House, 235 Old Ocean Road," replied David. A wealthy industrialist and businessman owned it. Mr. J. Robert Pennington donated it to New York City for a nursing home. The city uses a small amount of money for upkeep and improvements. The last time I visited my grandfather, there was electricity and indoor plumbing on some of the lower floors". The city wants to make everything modern," said grandfather.

"Mr. Pennington died a few years ago and had no airs. He married Miss Glades Barton. She died at a young age from a heart attack. They had no children."

We have to go to the west side of the building'" said David turning Danny-Boy. That is where carriages and sleds park. An old gentleman by the name of Jed looks after horses and gives them hay and water. He will probably have to wake up, Danny," laughed David.

An older gentleman greeted David and Hannah while driving to the carriage area. He showed them where to park the sled and carriage.

"Howdy." Dr. Kilmore, "Said Jed. He had a smiling face and sparkling eyes—his smile revealed gaps of yellow teeth clutching onto a pipe. David could smell alcohol and tobacco but was glad to see him. On his head was an old canvas hat with different stains and holes. He was slightly bent over, and his suspenders held raged pants topped with an old wool shirt and a ragged jacket. His hands are shaking like a leaf.

"Happy New Year, Jed," said David. I won't be a doctor until I get my license in June. David helped Hannah off of the seat platform.

"I want you to meet Miss Hannah Rose Zimmer. Next summer, we will be married," said David, proudly looking at Hannah.

"Howdy and pleased to meet ya," Jed said, tipping his hat. Fred lifted the boys and Lilly out of the sled.

"I also want you to meet Miss Lilly May Zimmer, Hannah's younger sister. The two little boys are Sam and Duff." You know Miss Naomi and Fred Gruen."

"Good to see all of you," said Jeb smiling.

"I will meet you in about three hours," said Frank, still in the sled. I am going to visit granny. Her house is a few blocks from here."

"Greet her for me," said David.

"I will have you come in the side door; said, Jeb. There is only one step. The front has five. Steps. Wait here, and I will get a wagon to hold your packages. Someone donated wagons and carts to the facility. The residents love it because they can carry books, laundry, grandchildren, or whatever they want." David and Naomi put the packages in a cart and wagon.

Miss Naomi guided the group into the building. David picked up the picnic basket.

They entered a small foyer and then a large room with smells of an oil stove and hardwood floors. Wallpaper in stripes and flowers accented with beige colors, pale yellow, and light brown add warmth to the room. Residents and nursing staff photos surround Mr. and Mrs. Pennington's large portrait on their wedding day. The high ceiling has a long chain supporting a light globe decorated with a crystal chandelier. Nurses and attendants carrying oil lamps mingled among the residents to care for their needs.

A sweet voice from a pretty middle-aged woman with rustling petticoats and a printed skirt topped with a crisp pink blouse welcomed the little group to Pennington House.

"Welcome, Naomi and Dr. Kilmore," said Barbara. Your grandfather is waiting for you. I have him in our day room with his friends. So you can introduce everyone when we get there."

"Do ghosts live here?" said Sam looking up at the high ceiling. "Yes, said Duff, they hide so you can.t see them."

"Sam looked at David, who was shaking his head. No, where did you get that idea?"

"The older boys tell the little kids ghosts and witches live in high places," added Lilly.

The Kilmore's followed Barbara into the cheerful day room. A cozy fireplace greeted them with dancing flames that looked like elves at a party. A long table in the center of the room, decorated with ten plates accompanied by napkins and silverware, is inviting. "I hope we have enough dishes for all of you," said Barbara, lighting the candles.

Lilly quickly counted everyone and said, "There are ten of us.

And ten plates on the table."

"Sam, you and Duff put the wagons over by the Christmas tree, said, David. We will open presents after lunch."

"Hannah, the tree lights are winking at us like the lights at the hotel." Said Duff pulling on Hannah's skirt. She put her hands on his shoulders and said they were saying welcome to the party."

"David, thank you for bringing your beautiful family to visit us." Said grandfather while embracing his grandson. Please introduce them to all of us."

David put Hannah's hand into his and said, "I would like to present Miss Hannah Rose Zimmer. We are engaged and plan to marry next summer.

'I also want you to meet Miss Lilly May Zimmer, Hannahs's younger sister."

Grandfather extended his hand to Hannah and Lilly and said, "thank you for coming here today."

"Hannah and Lilly, grandfather, is my father," said Naomi.

My older brother Daniel was the father of David."

"I think I was about three when he died from a horse and buggy accident. My mama Sarah Martin Kilmore died from a heart attack when I was five. I still remember her, said David fondly, looking at Naomi. Then auntie became my mama," The boys shook hands with grandfather and said, we are glad to meet you."

"I have three friends. I would like you to meet. Of course, David and Naomi know them." Said Mr. Kilmore, turning towards the men.

"In the first chair is Bill Miller, then Walt Simpson and Leonard Drake."

"Howdy, said the men smiling at Hannah, Lilly, Sam, and Duff.

"Your family is growing," said Bill, biting his pipe. You have added two young ladies and two children."

"Yes, " said Erick Kilmore, and I hope David and Hannah add to the family," looking at David with a twinkle.

Everyone seated themselves at the table. Naomi asked David to say grace. He asked everyone to join hands.

"Thank you, Heavenly Father, for this food and family gathering. Bless the food for the good of our bodies, and bless the hands who prepared it. AMEN.

Naomi served platers of plump sandwiches of turkey, ham, and roast beef accompanied by crystalline bowls of potato salad and fruit salad, followed by pumpkin pie, mincemeat, and apple pie. Naomi passed a basket of chunky oatmeal cookies piled to the brim. Short cups with handles are brimming with warm spiced apple cider.

"That was beautiful." Said Erick, wiping a tear from his eye. "David, I thought you were sitting by Sam.", said Hannah.

"I am sitting by him. I know where to find him said David, holding up a corner of the tablecloth. Sam, why are you under the table?"

"I dropped my natkin," said the small boy. There are a lot of feet under here."

David pulled Sam from under the table and sat him in his chair.

"Look at you said David to Sam. You are soaking wet from the neck down. "How did you get that wet, and what is on your shirt."

"The juice fell out of my cup, and now I have a wet shit.' "My shoe and sock are wet. I didn't know where the toilet

was, and everyone was talking."

"Sam, it is ok to interrupt an adult if you need something.

What is in your hair? It looks like a bunch of cookie crumbs." "Sam, let me wipe off my hands in his hair," said Duff. "Oh, me," said David.

"Don't' worry, David said. Hannah, you know I have a big bag of shoes and clothes for Sam. This time I added a washcloth and a towel."

"I will clean him up," said David. He put the bag of clothes on his shoulder. Where is the toilet?"

HANNAH

"Walk out into the hall, take the first left, and you will see both men and women," said Grandfather. He and his friends were shaking with laughter.

"Sam always comes home in different clothes, and then I have to wash everything, including him," laughed Hannah.

"While they are gone, the girls and I will stack these dishes and take them to the kitchen said Naomi," picking up some dishes.

"I will get a dish cart for you and take them to the kitchen," offered Walter.

David came back to the room carrying Sam, wrapped in a quilt.

"Sam, do you want to stand by the fireplace and keep warm?"

"No replied Sam. I want down."

The little boy went over to grandfather and said, "I went to the "toilet, then pulled the chain. I washed my hands. See, they are clean," said Sam holding out his hands.

"You are a big boy," said Erick, smiling.

"David is a big boy too. He went into the toilet, I pulled the chain, and he washed his hands."

Grandfather and his friends had a good laugh. Hannah and Lilly giggled.

"We better hand out the presents and get ready to leave," said David looking at his watch. I want to get everyone home before dark."

"Duff and Sam, I will hand you the present and tell you who to give it to," instructed Naomi.

"Duff, you take one to Leonard and one to Bill. Sam gives Walter and one to grandfather."

"I will show you how to open a present," said Sam to his great-grandfather.

"Okay, said Erick, you show all of us how to open a present." Sam is hanging on to the present; he says rip off the paper like this. Sam ripped the paper into two shreds and said, open the box. Oh, no, said Sam, you got a green vest. You didn't get a toy!" You got green gloves, a green and red scarf, and a red and green hat."

Counting on his fingers, Duff said, Mr. Walter got everything red and blue, and Mr. Bill got red and brown. Everyone got the same thing, a vest, hat, scarf, and gloves."

"Boys, pick up the ribbon and paper and put it in a basket near the fireplace. Thank you for doing that." Said Hannah.

"I will take the picnic basket out and tell Jeb we are almost ready to go home," said David.

"Don't forget there is a box of candy and cookies for each of you. I don't want the children to see the boxes, or they will want some." Said Hannah. "Everyone goes to the bathroom and puts your hat and coat on," reminded David.

"Duff, Sam, and Lilly, there is a small gift for you on the buffet." Said Leonard. Erick and Bill did the carving, and Walter and I did the painting." said Leonard Duff and Sam ran to the table. A herd of hand-carved and painted animals stood in rows.

"I want a cat like Miss Kitty," said Lilly. I found a black and white cat."

"I want a horse that looks like Danny, Boy said, Duff. I think I found one that looks like him".

"I want a dog that looks like Ring," said Sam choosing his toy. "Each of you can take home a bag of peppermint sticks and gumdrops." Said grandfather.

"You only get one gumdrop, now; save the rest for another day," cautioned Hannah. Hand me the sacks, and I will put them in my bag. You can play with your toy on the way home."

"I think Fred is here," said David looking out the window.

"I hope you don't mind," said Naomi. I want to visit my father some more and talk to his caregivers. I know he has some clothing I need to mend, and I want to ensure he has shaving cream, lotion, and soap. I will take the picnic basket. I have some other things to take home. Lilly and the children will have more room in the carriage."

"That is ok with me," said David. I will see you, maybe tomorrow?"

Naomi hugged everyone and said goodbye.

"Boys, I will take you to the bathroom right now. I don't want to make any stop on the way home," said David. Then we will say goodbye to everyone."

"Come on, Lilly," said Hannah, we should go to the lady's room."

"Goodbye, son," said Erick hugging David. Let me know when you get to school.

"Hannah and Lilly, Sam and Duff, it was a pleasure meeting you, and return soon."

Erick watched David climb up to the driving platform, take Hannah in his arms, and kiss her. There is something familiar about the name Zimmer, and their accent sounds like German, Thought Erick. I have heard a German accent around here."

Dave ensured the carriage doors were secure and everyone was comfortable, then climbed up to the driver's seat.

"Father is there anything I can get for you," Naomi took Erick's hand. The elderly man smiled and said," what a beautiful family you brought me. Hannah and Lilly look like angels. The little fellows, Duff and Sam, are entertaining. Sam is busy and gets into everything. Duff laughs at Sam. Then I start to laugh. It is a treat when children come to visit. , they fill the gap of loneliness."

"Now, my beautiful blushing rose. We have some time together," said David taking Hannah into his arms and kissing her.

"I made New Year's Eve dinner reservations at the Atlantic side Hotel. The choices were six pm or eight pm. I took the six pm reservation. The orchestra will start at about eight, and we will dance the night away. We have a busy new year, graduation, wedding, and house fixing. I will kiss you into the new year," said David, smiling at Hannah. She rested her head on David's shoulder, closed her eyes, and thought about magical nights and lovely stars.

THE NEW YEAR

CHAPTER 13

"I hear a knock at the door," said Lilly. David must be here. Where are the two of you going at eight in the morning?" asked Lilly. I will open the door for your handsome prince. Are you two going to kiss?"

"I hope so," said Hannah looking in the mirror.

"Good morning Hannah and Lilly," said David. Where is Sam?"

Duff wanted him to s spend the night with him and his sisters," said Hannah.

"Lilly, we are to have breakfast with Naomi at her home. Then we will look at the old farmhouse where David grew up. David said I could choose the paint and wallpaper. We have a lot of planning to do".

David helped Hannah put on her coat and purse. I will be back late this afternoon."

"I feel lost without Sam and his dry clothes bag," said Hanna as she Climbed up to the carriage platform.

David and Hannah stepped into Naomi's kitchen to smell ham, waffles, and scrambled eggs.

"This kind of breakfast is a treat." Said Hannah.

"Thank you, said Naomi, pouring tea for Hannah and coffee for David.

"What are your plans for today?" asked Naomi.

"Well, said David while taking another waffle. I am taking Hannah to the old farmhouse to approve our future home. We are dressed warm and have lanterns, so we should be able to see almost everything."

"Thank you, Naomi, for breakfast, said Hannah. You will have to show me how to make waffles. I will have two boys and one man to cook for."

"Have a good time searching the old place, said Naomi. It has been a long time since I have been in our childhood house."

Hannah and David walked thru the soft snow carrying lanterns and a lamp to their future home.

"We will go into the house from the back door, said David. I swept the stairs and the porch. Be careful. There are loose boards on the two stairs and porch."

Hannah gazed at the steeply pitched roof resting under its blanket of snow, accented in palest blue colors contrasted with deepest blue gables, canopied over windows and doors.

David opened the squeaky screen door, unlocked it, and pushed open the heavy back door. He motioned Hannah to walk into the service porch. She noticed ample cupboards and shelves that store jars of fruit and vegetables.

The porch has familiar odors that remind Hannah of the big farmhouse in Germany. Before opening another entry door into the kitchen, Hannah noticed a dainty spider spinning her web in the ceiling's corner, trying to make ends meet. The dark, damp rooms didn't give Hannah a feeling of home.

However, Hannah did visualize young David running thru the rooms. A comical wood stove with a dented tea kettle on top leaned on the hot water tank. Hannah could imagine the tempting stews and bubbling soups that presided over the top of the stove.

David set the lamp he was carrying on the plank of the solid maple kitchen table. The scratches and dents told the families' stories that it had served the initials "DK" neatly carved on the end of the table.

"What is behind that door by the sink?" asked Hannah.

"It is the door to the pantry, replied David. You can look inside if you care to. I am going to take a look at the hot water tank. I hope it doesn't fall over."

Hannah cautiously opened the pantry door. David hears her scream.

"What's the matter, Hannah? Did you hurt yourself?"

"NO! Said Hannah. I just saw a mouse run across the floor!" "I will get a shovel or broom and smack him," said David.

"I don't want you to hurt him, said Hannah. I want you to make him go away."

"What do you want me to do?" laughed David, shaking hands with him.?"

"David, you are silly, said Hannah. Cleaning up this kitchen will take a lot of scrubbing and disinfectant."

"Let's look at the dining room," suggested David. I think you will like it. The table has room for twelve people. We have to refinish it. Most of the furniture in the hose has to be refinished, repaired, or replaced. We will get it done. The first thing I want to do is wire the house for electricity and install indoor plumbing."

"Won't that be expensive?" remarked Hannah.

"Yes, said David. I will talk to you about the budget and expenses. We can keep track using the calendars and notebooks auntie gave us."

"I like the stair banister and winding staircase," said Hannah running her fingers over the smooth wood. Is that a closet underneath the stairs?"

"Yes, said David. The plumbing contractor suggested we put in a toilet and basin. That will keep the children out of our bedroom and bathroom."

"Follow me, said David. Our room will be the large bedroom to the right. I will add a full bathroom at the plumber's suggestion." "That is what I call luxury, said Hannah. I was going to be happy with a bathroom under the stairs."

David pushed the door open to the main bedroom. "I can't remember if it was my mother or grandmother that added an addition to this room," said David opening the dusty curtains.

HANNAH

"There are so many closets and shelves here," said Hannah. I like the four-poster bed."

"We will have to refinish the headboard and footboard and replace the mattress. In addition, we need new sheets, pillows, and blankets," said David.

"Did you wet this bed, David?" asked Hannah, laughing.

"I remember jumping on the bed and having pillow fights with "my grandfather. Grandmother would not let any of the kids jump on her bed. We had to bathe before she let us sleep in bed. Yes, I think I did wet the bed a time or two. Grandfather said he would not tell me. There will be a bathroom on that long wall with a closet .when it becomes our bedroom," said David admiring Hannah.

"Can I see the living room?" asked Hannah.

"Follow me, and I will take you there." Said David, still looking at Hannah.

My beautiful maternal grandmother Sara Martin is the picture on the wall in the hallway. The Martin farmhouse is not very far from here. The Martins are from my mother's side of the family. I can still hear the noise of us kids running through the house. Hannah had to walk through the dining room to get to the living room. A beam of twirling sunlight streamed thru the tall narrow window and danced on the dining table. Hannah could hear the laughter and joy of the Kilmore and Martin families in the chambers of her heart. She vision young David sitting by his grandfather at the dining table.

"I love this large living room. It looks big enough for a party, said Hannah. The fireplace is beautiful. I like the opening from the living room to the dining room. Everyone can enjoy the fireplace from either room."

"Who painted the lovely seascape over the living room fireplace?" asked Hannah

"Grandmother Martin painted it," said David proudly.

"I will take you upstairs, said David leading the way. There are five bedrooms. The plumbing contractor said he could turn one of the bedrooms into a bathroom at the end of the hall." We can ask the boys if they want separate bedrooms or share one."

"They have always shared a room with someone, said Hannah. When they get used to this big house, they may want separate bedrooms. Duff will keep his bedroom neat. Sam will be a disaster." said Hannah. She looked up at the tall walls and high ceilings upstairs. She also noticed neighboring spiders making their home in the high corners and a few cobwebs clinging to the window curtains. How will I keep these rooms clean? Hannah thought to herself. Hannah had an overwhelming feeling about the tasks before her. How could she be a wife and mother, cook meals, and care for a house and garden? I don't know where to start. How do I plan a wedding when I have never been to one?

"I have an idea said, Hannah. Where are you taking me to lunch?"

"We can go to the city and have lunch at the Atlantic Room restaurant, or Jordan's sandwich shop is not too far from here," replied David.

"Jordan's is fine with me, said Hannah. I like their soup and sandwiches."

"Danny Boy can catch up on his sleep while we are there," said David.

Hannah and David walked into Jordan's restaurant to the spicy fragrance of chicken, apple pie, and other pastries.

"Good afternoon Dr. Kilmore and Hannah," said Mrs. Jordan. Would you like to sit by a window?" "Yes, thank you said, David.

"May I bring you something to drink?" said Mrs. Jordan handing the couple a menu.

"Yes, said David, Hannah would like tea and coffee with cream for me.

"I want your toasted cheese sandwich and chicken vegetable soup," said Hannah looking at the menu.

"I will have a medium steak and fried potatoes," said David. "Hannah, you look troubled. Is there anything I can do?" said

David stirring his coffee.

HANNAH

"Oh, no said Hannah smiling. The house is so big. How will we ever get it fixed the way we want It.?"

"One room or project at a time said David gently. I have contractors for electricity and plumbing. We will finish the kitchen, our bedroom, and one for the boys. I will be working two jobs for a while, part-time at the livery stable and full-time at the veterinarian clinic. I have my inheritance from my grandfather saved, and I have other money saved. We can hire some painters and wallpaper hangers. I will make sure your kitchen and pantry are mouse-proof."

"I am going to love being your wife, said Hannah. By the way, I want some apple pie with cream on it."

Mrs. Jordan brought the couple apple pie, tea, and coffee. I hope I can learn to make an apple pie as well as you and Aunt Naomi," said Hannah.

You will learn, said Mrs. Jordan. I didn't always know how to cook. I am thankful my husband was patient with me. That's how you learn. You try things on your husband and children," laughed Mrs. Jordan walking away from the table.

"David, I need to ask a favor of you," said Hannah smiling. When you pay the bill, will you get the boys some candy? I saw jars of gumdrops and chocolate by the cash register."

"And where are you going?" said David sipping his coffee. "I will be in the ladies' room," said Hannah.

Mary Beth and Mrs. Jordan said goodbye to Hannah and David.

"Oh, David, I will see you at the college parties and dances." "Yes, said David, Hannah will be at all the dances and parties with me."

Mary Beth watched David and Hannah walk hand in hand to their carriage through tears. She could see them laughing and talking. David picked up Hannah, placed her on the driver's platform, leaned over, and kissed her.

"Betsy, you have to get over David. He loves Hannah, and she loves him. You are a smart, attractive young woman; you will find your true love. They love each other. There is nothing you can do to change that. Don't you want a husband that loves you as much as you love him?"

"Yes, said Betsy wiping her nose. I would be happy if David loved me just a little bit. I have enough love for both of us."

Mary Beth, you know love doesn't work that way. Love is a full partnership. So dry your tears and start planning your senior year as a nursing student. Go to the parties and dances that the college will have."

"I'll plan for my future. It won't be what I want. I want David."
"The best thing you can do, Betsy, is helping me prepare for the dinner shift."

"Hannah, I forgot to tell you I have my school schedule. David took a long envelope out of his jacket pocket. Do you have your calendar with you?"

"Yes, said Hannah, opening up her purse.

: You will see I start classes on Monday the fifteenth of January. The following weekend will be a "winter Dace. Will you be my date?" said David looking at Hannah.

"I would love to put on a pretty dress and go with you, said Hannah writing on the calendar.

On Wednesday, the thirteenth, is the final registration. You can come with me, and we can visit my grandfather, "said David. After that, there will be another schedule with parties and activities. You can come to the school on those weekends. I will make a copy of the schedule for you."

"I will be busy planning our wedding," remarked Hannah. Do you think Miss Naomi will advise us on the house and the wedding?"

"Yes, said David. She would give opinions on almost everything. Don't worry about the house. You can choose the paint colors and wallpaper. We also have to plan our honeymoon."

WEDDING PLANS

CHAPTER 14

"David" is here!" shouted Sam while running up the stairs to let Hannah and Lilly know of the arrival of David and Danny Boy. Can I open the door and bring him in?"

Lilly opened her bedroom door, and there they were, David and Sam, both smiling. Sam wanted to go for a piggyback ride and hugged and kissed David.

"Sam, I want you to calm down. All of us will spend this Saturday afternoon together at Miss Naomi's, have lunch and talk about the wedding," said David

Go and get Duff and the two of you put on your hat, coat, gloves, overshoes, and scarves," said David. Let's all go downstairs and get everyone in the carriage."

"Sam, tell Duff and the girls to get in the carriage," said Hannah

"I will count everyone," volunteered Lilly. We have David, Hannah, and me. That is three of us. Gwen and Allison, Duff and Sam".

"What's a wedding? "Sam asked Lilly.

"It's a party where people get married," said Lilly adjusting Sam's hat and scarf.

"You and Duff are invited. Miss Naomi will tell us about it. "Will there be cookies today?" asked Duff.

"Yes said, Lilly. There will be cookies today and at the wedding. David made sure everyone was safely in the carriage and closed the doors. Then, he took his place beside Hannah on the

driving platform. He stole a kiss, and she did the same.

"When will you get there?" said Sam hugging his toy cat. I want to play with Miss Kitty."

"I want to play with Ring," said Duff hugging his toy dog. "Oh-oh said Sam to Lilly. I have to go to the toilet." "Can't you wait?" said Lilly; we are almost to Naomi's. "No said Sam; it is coming!"

Gwen, Duff, and Allyson tried to move away from Sam, but it was too late.

I'll knock on the window and see if I can get attention from Hannah or David." said Lilly.

"What's that knocking noise on the window?" said Hannah. "I know for sure what it is, said David. Sam has wet his

drawers. I didn't take him to the bathroom before we left, did you?"

"No said, Hannah. I was thinking about other things.

"There is an open space up ahead. We will stop there and change Sam before he gets icicles on his butt mused David. He guided Danny to a level place.

Hannah picked up her dry clothes bag and asked David," do you want to undress or dress him?"

"I will undress him while you get out of the clothes. I hope his shoes aren't wet."

Soon Sam was dry, and David guided Danny Boy to Naomi's back door.

David jumped off of the diving platform, giving Hannah a helping hand. He opened the carriage door and said to the kids, "When you get inside Auntie's back porch, take off your overshoes and place them on the rug she has provided. Boys don't run through the house. Use your best manners and indoor voice."

"Ok," said Sam

"I won't run said, Duff.

Naomi was at the back door giving hugs and kisses.

Hello, Gwen and Allison. I haven't seen you for a while. Welcome. Where is Junie?"

"She was adopted by a young couple moving out west. She said it would be the first time in a private home. We are so happy for her and miss her," said Gwen.

"We can't run in the house, and we have to take off our overshoes," said Sam

"That would be lovely," said a smiling Naomi. Ring and Miss Kitty are taking a nap by the fireplace. Both of you can go and pet them. Then wash your hands," instructed Naomi

The two boys went into the living room to see their pets. Sam was trying not to run.

"Miss Kitty, I am here to play with you."

Sam petted the head of the sleeping cat. She opened one eye, looked at Sam, yawned, and went back to sleep.

The ring couldn't give both boys enough wet kisses and whimpers for attention and love.

"Wake up, Miss Kitty," said Sam. I want to play with you".

She ignored Sam and snuggled down in her basket.

"Naomi, Miss Kitty won't wake up and play. Ring will play." "She won't?" said David. I will see if I can wake her up."

David went into the living room, knelt, and petted the lazy cat. She said, meow, and went back to her nap.

"I am sorry she doesn't want to play. Maybe she is waiting for lunch. You watch; when she smells the food on the table, she will get up and sit under your chair."

"David, how come she won't play? Is she mad at me.?"

No, said David. Cats do what they want to do. They don't try to please you the way dogs do. Ring wanted to play as soon as he saw you, boys. Dogs like to please and are very loyal. I hear auntie calling us for lunch. I will take the two of you to the bathroom so you can wash your hands."

"Davidid, I only used one hand to pet her. So I don't have to wash both of them."

"How are you going to that?" asked David ushering the boys to the bathroom.

I will splash my hand in the water and shake it to dry.

"I will wash both hands," said David opening the bathroom door. Don't you want to do it the way I do.?"

"Okay. Davidid, I will do it." Replied the small boy.

"Ladies, I will ladle the chicken rice soup into bowls, and you can set them on the table. I have put some soup in cups for the children. And it has cooled."

Naomi handed Gwen a heaping platter of thick roast beef sandwiches to put on the table.

"Where do you want us to sit?" inquired Allison.

"David and I sit at either end of the table, with Hannah next to him. Duff can sit by Hannah and Sam next to David."

"Thanks, auntie," said David with a smile. 'David, will y please say the blessing?"

"Yes said David; everyone joined hands. Then, David bowed his head and recited the blessing he had known from childhood taught to him by his grandfather.

"Heavenly Father, thank you for this family gathering. And all of your blessings.

Bless the food for the good of our bodies, and bless everyone here and the hands who made it. We ask these things in the name of Jesus Amen.'

"Naomi, I love this chicken noodle soup. But, you will have to show me how to make it," Hannah took another bite.

"I am collecting family recipes for you. I will mark the ones David likes. I can't keep a secret. I would give it to you as a wedding gift. So you come over any time to cook, and we will practice on David." Said Naomi smiling.

"I will meet the challenge said David taking another bite of his sandwich. He heard Oh!! David put his sandwich on his plate and turned to Sam. You didn't——."

"No said Sam; here comes Miss Kitty. She has her big tail up in the air," said Sam giggling.

"Where else is she going to put it?" Duff asked. "Now she is under my chair," laughed Sam. "Ring is sitting by David," mused Allison.

"After lunch, you boys can feed the animals their lunch," said Naomi.

"What are they going to have?" asked Duff.

"I have a large beef bone saved for Ring and some chicken for Miss Kitty. But don't worry, they never go to Hungary," said Naomi.

"Boys, look out the window. It is starting to snow. Would you like to make a snowman after lunch?" asked David.

"Yes! Said Duff and Sam in unison.

I want both boys to use the bathroom before we play,' said" David.

"David, I don't have to use the bathroom," said Sam

"Yes, you do," said David. If you get your drawer wets, you will have ice cycles on your butt."

"Okay, Davidid," said the small boy.

"Ladies, the four of us can finish the dishes fast. I am glad David is playing with the boys. He is still a big kid!" remarked Naomi

"You ladies have fun talking about the wedding and other things women talk about," said David, closing the service porch door.

"Don't worry, David, we will call you when we need money," teased Hannah.

Miss Naomi, where do you want us to put the dried dishes?" said Allison sweetly.

You can put them in the pantry. You will see where everything goes." Answered

Naomi.

"I am glad the dishes are out of the way; thank you all for helping. I will get out some notes about weddings." Have any of you ladies been to a wedding? Everyone responded, NO' "

A wedding is a ceremony where two people are married. The reception is a party for the bride and groom after the ceremony." You know, weddings are one of the ways I make a living. I make dresses for the bridesmaids and the bridal gown and veil. I also help design the invitations. We can sit around the dining room table. And look at notes and pictures. Hannah, I am giving you a notebook about planning a wedding. I don't have time to make a copy for everyone; you can make your copy if you want to. I have enough paper and pens for everyone. We aren't going to plan all of the weddings today. I want to help Hannah and David know where to begin. Hannah, on the first page of your notebook, you will notice it says where to start. There are three things you need to consider right now. First, make a guest list of everyone you want to invite. That will help you determine the church size and reception room. Set a date for the marriage. Then you choose the bridal party. Lilly will be the bride's maid of honor, Allison, and Gwen, the bridesmaids. Finally, you can select the colors for

The girl's dresses. Some brides choose two coordinating colors, and some choose three.

"I think I have enough fabric that you can choose from the bolts of material in the attic and my sewing room, and at my dress shop, I will make the dresses and the bridal gown and veil.

"I just heard a snowball hit the house," said Naomi. It was Sam," said everyone in unison.

"Can we keep our dress, or do we give it back?" inquired Allison.

"You will keep them, and they will be a nice reminder of the wedding of David and Hannah."

The girls heard a noise on the service porch; the boys were coming inside the house. They heard David instruct the boys to take off their boots and keep on their shoes.

Sam and Duff walked into the dining room full of smiles, rosy cheeks, and runny noses.

: We had fun, said, Duff. So when do we get our desert?"

"Go and wash your hands, and I made you some hot chocolate," said Naomi walking into the kitchen.

"Did all of you have fun?" asked Hannah.

"Yes, said Sam and Duff. Ring knocked over our snowman." David came into the dining room with rosy cheeks and smiling.

But, unfortunately, we have to leave soon. I want everyone to be home before it is dark." said David.

"Auntie, do you have some hot coffee?"

"I always have coffee when you are around," said Naomi. "Hannah. Do you know how to plan a wedding?" asked David sipping his coffee.

"Well, said Hannah, I know where to start. But, thanks to Naomi, I feel more confident that things will get done."

"On the way home, you can tell me about it," smiled David. "Duff and Sam, I will ask you to sit at the kitchen table to eat your dessert." Said, David.

"I want cake and cookies," said Duff.

"I want cookies and pie," said Sam.

"You can eat your cookies on the way home. Now you have finished your dessert. After that, you can give the animals their lunch, and treat, said David; then I want you boys to use the bathroom just before leaving."

Sam looked at David and then said, ok, Davdid."

"Thank you for lunch," said Gwen. It will be fun to get a new dress."

"Thank you, Miss Naomi," said Allison while buttoning her coat and putting on her gloves. I love to come here," she added.

"Thank you said, Lilly. I will have fun helping to make the dresses," she smiled: Thank you for telling me how to get started on the wedding.

I don't feel so lost now," said Hannah looking at David.

"When do we start making the dresses?" asked Allison.

"As soon as Hannah chooses the dress patterns and fabric."Said Naomi. Why don't you girls come over next week after school? We will make the selections at that time,"

"Everyone into the carriage," said David trying to get the girls on their way.

"Guess what? Said Sam; I used the bathroom." "So did! I," said Duff jumping up and down.

"We will get out of your way so you can have a peaceful afternoon," said David hugging his aunt.

"It means more to me than you will ever know," said Naomi choking back a tear. It will be too quiet. I am glad to have Miss Kitty and Ring keep me company."

David helped Hannah onto the carriage's driving platform, stole a kiss from her, and signaled Danny to wake up and get going!

"Hannah tells me about our wedding plans," said David. You seem more confident now than you did a few hours ago."

"Well," said Hannah pulling her shawl closer around her, I have learned something new from you and auntie."

"What is that?" inquired David.

"When we talked about all the work and money it will take to remodel the house, I thought, how will we ever get that done? You said one room or one project at a time. We don't have to do it all at once. Auntie said we start planning the wedding from the beginning. We first have to make a guest list and decide how many people to invite, then choose a church and set a date."

"Speaking of a church," said David, will you go to eight o'clock mass with me tomorrow morning at The Chapel of the Rose? It is in the Village of the Blushing Rose, close to Martin Farm and other farms nearby. Sometimes I attend mass there instead of going to the city at St Mark's Cathedral near the Atlantic Side Hotel."

"Why is it called The Village of the Blushing Rose?" asked Hannah.

"There is a unique climbing rose in red, pink, and sometimes lavender colors. They are as beautiful as you," said David.

"Maybe I could get a rose to grow in my flower garden," commented Hannah.

"I am sure you will have roses and other flowers in your garden," smiled David.

"I will take you to the village after church tomorrow morning." "Yes, David, I will go to mass with you tomorrow. We need to spend all of the time alone together. January fifteen is getting closer."

"I always have breakfast after communion," said David. So we will have breakfast together also."

"It is getting cold and dark. I better get everyone safely home," said David signaling Danny-Boy to go faster.

When David got home, he noticed Naomi had no lumps. The house was eerily dark. He could hear Ring barking. When he entered the service porch, he saw Naomi sitting at the dining room table.

"What is the matter, auntie? You look like you have seen a ghost."

"I have seen a ghost. Naomi replied, a ghost of my past. Take the lamp up to the attic, and you will see what I am talking about,"

"Do you want me to come up with me?" asked David.

Naomi dried her eyes and wiped her nose. You lead the way, David." Said Naomi standing up and walking toward the long flight of stairs. I left the attic door open, so you can see what I am talking about," sniffed Naomi handing the lamp to David.

"I could have gone up to the attic and got whatever you are looking for," said David. You seldom go up there."

David took Naomi's arm, and the two shadows ascended the stairs. When they reached the top landing, David saw that the attic door was partly open. He let go of Naomi's arm and pushed the door open the rest of the way.

"Oh, no," said David holding the lamp on what was upsetting Naomi.

"That is me, said Naomi, tears flowing. I had taken off the sheet that protected the dress from dust.

"Auntie, is that your wedding gown you made about fifteen years ago?"

"Yes, I feel like I am nothing more than the dress form it rests on. I feel I am wrapped in a shroud of sorrow. That's the dress that will never go down the aisle. I feel like an inanimate object without life."

.I loved William so much. Why did God take him from me?"
"Let's sit down and talk about this for a minute. Did you come up here to look at the dress?" said David in a low gentle voice.

He guided Naomi to a chair and pulled up one next to her. "You haven't told me why you came up here. You know I would get whatever you were looking for," said David.

"I came up here to find some fabric for the bridesmaid's dresses. Some women collect jewelry. I contain material, said Naomi wiping her eyes with her handkerchief.

"You have come up here to store things or look for something. You didn't seem bothered by the dress," said David.

"I know, said Naomi. I would blow a kiss on the dress and forget what I came up to get. Our engagement picture fell over. How did that happen?"

David set the lamp on a nearby table, picked up the picture, and handed it to Naomi. She pressed the image to her bosom.

The lamp cast shadows on Naomi's face. The side in the light was her happy, loving self, and the other showed great pain and longing in the dark clouds of sadness.

"Did you make the dress?" asked David.

"Yes, replied Naomi. I spent over a year designing and making the dress. I saved my money for the best silk, Satin, and lace. I fashioned my cathedral-length silk veil held by a crown of satin roses with accents of pearls. Graceful long tapered sleeves held up an off-shoulder neckline accented with a satin and pearl rose. "The accident happened on August nineteenth. On Saturday, August twenty-second, we planned to be married in St Mark's Cathedral near The Atlantic Side Hotel 'where we planned to have the reception. I had to have the right kind of gown and veil to go with the church," smiled Naomi.

"Tell me about William," said David, ready to listen. I remember him slightly."

"As you know, began Naomi, drying a tear. His name was William Ashton Marshall, the third. He was born in Northwestern, Pennsylvania. He and his parents, two younger brothers, and a younger sister moved to Brooklyn to a farm near the city'; David was nine or ten. William went to law school in Brooklyn. His father and grandfather were attorneys; William followed them. Will was a general practice lawyer for farmers and anyone that needed legal counsel. He would start his law practice in the city like you create your animal practice. We would live in this house, and I would keep my dressmaking business. Both of us love children and were eager to start a family.

"Everything was perfect, said Naomi taking a deep breath. Like you, we had careers and were deeply in love. The two of you remind me of William and myself. There will never be another man in my life who I could love the way I still love him. And then it happened," said Naomi softly "You mean the accident?" asked David gently

"Yes, said Naomi blowing her nose. I was to meet William at Grand Central Station. He would be on the four-thirty pm train coming from Brooklyn. He was on a business trip and wanted to meet with some friends he lived with at Mrs. Keepers Boarding House. At five pm, the train was not there. The train clerk told everyone that this train is sometimes late because it makes several stops before it arrives at the station. I began to panic because the train was not there by six pm. We heard there had been an accident. There are no details. We got the news of a head-on collision between a passenger and a freight train. It was twelve-thirty when we got the passenger list of those killed."

"I knew Will was injured or dead. He liked to visit with the conductor and engineer. The passengers in the first few cars were badly injured or killed. After that, almost everyone had an injury." "We were to be married in a few days. What was I supposed

to do? On August twenty-second? The funeral was at St Mark's Cathedral five days later. And he is buried in St James Catholic Cemetery in Brooklyn. I have visited the cemetery a few times. I get depressed and cry for days. I can't believe he is gone." "Auntie, may I ask you one more question? How did the two of you meet?"

Naomi took a deep breath, wiped her eyes, and smiled slightly. At a tag dance at the Atlantic Side Hotel. His date was a girl named Virginia. My date was Steve Bradley. I felt warm and tingly in Will's arms while dancing. We held each other close. After that, we dated, and he graduated from law school. He lived in a run-down old boarding house near here and was looking forward to living in this house. I still have some of his possessions that he brought over."

"David, I want to show you something sniffed Naomi. See those shelves with a sheet over them to the right of you. Would you take the sheet off to see what is on the shelves?"

David removed the sheet and said, "Good grief, it looks like a fabric store. There are ribbons, buttons, and other things on these shelves."

"I have some lovely shades of pink from deepest to palest pink and prints and plaids. Some of the fabric is silk taffeta, silk, and matte satin. Shades of lavender look nice with some pink, and I have silver colors. Hannah would like to choose her bridesmaids' dresses from this collection. I have a few patterns and a catalog; she can look through some patterns to decide her style. I can sketch a dress if she doesn't like the patterns."

"Oh, David, I will not charge you for the fabric, " said Naomi. I have three employees who help with dressmaking, and I have several weddings and party dresses to make. I will ask Lilly if she wants to learn the art of dressmaking. She is a natural, and I will pay her."

"David, I am glad we had this conversation. I don't know what came over me. I better get supper started before it gets too late," said Naomi looking at her watch.

"Auntie, the only way you will get out of the dark is to look for the light."

Weeping may end for a night. Psalms 30.5

THE VILLAGE

CHAPTER 15

"Hannah, you look beautiful this Sunday morning. What time did you get up? I know that you are a late sleeper," said David helping Hannah onto the driving platform of the carriage. Danny Boy snorted and shook his head, letting David know he was in a happy frisky mood.

"I got up at six-fifteen, so I would be ready to go to communion at eight o'clock," yawned Hannah.

"I know you will enjoy the mass, and I will show you around The Village of the Rose. Unfortunately, we won't have lunch until the Drug Store's lunch counter opens at eleven. Most of the stores are closed on Sunday. A few places open after church services."

Hannah sat close to David and wrapped her shawl around her shoulders. The cold icy wind made Hannah snuggle with David. He gave her a quick kiss on her forehead.

"Hannah, we will go up a hill and around an S-shaped curve to the village entrance. Get ready for Danny to go thru a mud
 puddle at the bottom of the mountain. There is a level place to pull over. We can look down at the village.

David parked the carriage where Danny could nibble on some grass. He took Hannah's hand and helped her climb down the driving platform. He kissed her passionately and said to Hannah Rose, " I love you so much."

"..David, this is a lovely view. It almost seems magical," said Hannah with excitement.

"In a way, it is, said David. The blushing rose will only grow here. Some gardeners think the soil is fertile, and others say the roses get the right amount of sunlight all year.

Hand in hand, the young couple gazed at the kingdom below them. The soft morning light filled the valley with lovely morning shadows

"David, I hear church bells ringing in the distance."

"That means we have fifteen minutes before mass begins. We better hurry."

"Did you enjoy the service and Father Marks's message?" said David to Hannah.

"Yes, said Hannah, I enjoy hearing stories of the bible. I knew what was going on during the mass. Remember, I live in a Catholic Orphanage."

"I didn't know Naomi would be here; let's go and say hello to her," suggested Hannah.

"Hi, kids, said Miss Naomi. David, be sure and introduce Hannah to Father Mark."

"Are you staying for coffee?' inquired Naomi.

"No said, David. I am going to show Hannah around the village. Then we will have lunch at The Drug Store."

"I have to leave now, and I am in a hurry; said, Naomi. By the way, Hannah, I have ideas for the wedding. You can come over at any time. Remember, they are ideas. You are the bride, so you get to choose what you want."

"Auntie knows everyone here, and you can be sure some folks will be on the wedding invitation list," remarked David.

"Father Mark, I want you to meet my finance, Miss Hann Rose Zimmer."

"Welcome to Rose Chapel," smiled the Father, extending his hand to Hannah.

"It is a pleasure to meet you," said Hannah.

"Would the two of you like to join us in the fellowship hall for refreshments?"

"Yes, said Hannah, a cup of tea sounds good. thankyou

"We will ride around the village until the Drug Store opens, said David, patting Hannah's hand while sipping his coffee and dunking his cookie.

"I am looking forward to it," said Hannah, " I am starving."

"We will ride thru the main street first. Then we will look at the houses and barns."

Vast meadows of orchards and unfenced flocks stretched eastward. Wandering over the fields, the Rose River gives the village nourishment, substance, and means. Its tributary branched to the estuary flowing eastward and southward. The primordial forest provided shade with madrone trees bending to the river. The farms reposed red barns with their lofts and black trim accenting the white houses and gabled roofs stretching over the doors. David and Hannah saw Church steeples in the distance towards the most profound Blue Mountains.

"David, why are there so many sheep? What do they do with them?"

"The sheep are raised for their wool. First, the village women spin the yarn. Then, they take the thread to the city to sell. Sometimes, a small yarn shop is open in the summer. I think auntie has grandmother Martins spinning wheel."

"I don't think I would like to sit and spin yarn on a spinning wheel. I wouldn't say I want to knit. I make mistakes that Lilly or Naomi has to take apart and fix. Embroidery is something I am interested in. I would instead plant a vegetable garden and a flower garden. I am also anxious to sand and varnish furniture. That sounds like more fun," commented Hannah.

"It is almost eleven o'clock. It is time to get to the drugstore. There may be a line." Said, David.

"I am willing to wait in line if I have to," laughed Hannah. "I will park Danny next to some water," said David

The young couple climbed off the carriage platform and entered the drugstore. They opened the door, and a cheery bell announced their presence.

"It is busy," said David looking through the tables and counter. If that is ok with you, Hannah, I see two places at the counter."

"I don't think I have ever sat at a counter, said Hannah. As long as there is food, I am ok."

The couple sat at the counter and read the menu.

"They don't have many choices in small places like this, but the food is good." Said, David.

"What would you like, Hannah?" said David.

"I will have the beef stew with a toasted cheese sandwich and a hot cup of tea."

"I will order the same with coffee," said David.

"It's nice in here said Hannah, looking around. We can watch ourselves eat in those big mirrors across the counter. The hanging pictures are nice also."

"Do you want some ice cream?" said David. "Yes said Hannah, I want vanilla."

The couple left the Drug Store And climbed onto the carriage. Danny-Boy was munching on weeds, and David gave him sugar for a treat.

Hannah rested her head on David's shoulder and said I am so sad we only have about five days together you are leaving for school. I don't know what I would do without you".

"You won't have to be without me, said David tenderly. I will be home on Friday afternoon, and we will have the weekend together. Then, before we know it, spring break will be here. First, there are several spring dances and parties, and we can go to them. Time will go by fast," assured David.

"You are right, David," said Hannah cheering up. So where are we going?"

"I have one more place to show you, replied David. We are going to the beach.

The couple walked arm in arm to the ocean's noisy grotto, accented with the haunting moan of the Atlantic.

OFF TO COLLEGE

CHAPTER 16

"Hannah, you are so sad today." Said Lilly brushing Hannah's hair.

"I am sad because this is the day David leaves for college. I won't see him every day.

"When will he come home?" asked Lilly.

'He will be home on Friday afternoon. I miss him already."

"Hannah, you have to stop feeling sorry for yourself. Today is Saturday, and he will be gone for a few days. How is he getting to school?"

"Naomi is coming with us and driving the carriage back to her house. David is going on the four o'clock streetcar. They should be here any minute. David is taking me to lunch at the streetcar station, and we will spend the rest of the time together.

There was a knock at the door, and David greeted Hannah with a kiss. The ride was short to the streetcar.

"I have a suggestion that would work for all of us, said Naomi stepping out of the carriage

"It is one o'clock now. Why don't you kids have lunch, take a stroll through the park, and we meet here at three-thirty?"

"Auntie, what are you doing for the next couple of hours?" inquired David.

"There are shops near the wharf," said Naomi. I might find some fabric or lace and ribbon. I am always looking for something on sale," laughed Naomi.

David and Hannah looked at each other, smiled, and agreed it was a good plan.

"I will see you at three-thirty," said Naomi smiling and waving goodbye to David and Hannah.

"What do you want to do first, a walk or lunch?" said David taking Hannah's hand.

"You know me, said Hannah laughing; I want to go to lunch first."

"Do you want to sit at the lunch counter or a booth," asked David.

"I think a booth is more private," laughed Hannah. "Hannah, I don't want you to be sad or worried while I am away," David held Hannah's hand.

It isn't that, said Hannah. On the contrary, I will miss being with you, you talking to me, and you taking me to lunch," teased Hannah.

David and Hannah enjoyed their lunch of sandwiches and Coca-Cola at a nearby café.

"Let's walk in the park and down towards the shops, suggested David "Next Saturday, we will be together, said David. I think the school is about two miles from where my grandfather lives. "I am not that far away."

"I know said Hannah looking up at David and smiling. I will be busy with school and looking forward to my graduation, and I will help Naomi with the wedding plans.

"She is just the one helping you. The wedding is all about the bride," said David.

"Would you like to do some shopping or just walk thru the park?" asked David.

"I would like to look at the gardens and enjoy the day's beauty," said Hannah. Let's find a soda fountain. This time, I want chocolate said, Hannah.

HANNAH

The young couple sat under a naked maple tree and enjoyed their ice cream.

When they returned to the bus station, David and Hannah saw Naomi sitting at the lunch counter, drinking coffee and reading a magazine.

She looked at the couple, put down her coffee, and said, "David, do you have your bus ticket? There are a lot of people here.

"Yes, said David patting his breast pocket, I am ready." "I picked up some bus schedules for us," said Naomi.

"I am going outside; wait by the carriage, and give Danny some sugar." Said Naomi putting her magazine and schedules in her purse. You two find a private place to say goodbyes."

David took Hannah's arm, guided her to a tree's shadow, took her in his arms, and passionately kissed her goodbye. Hannah could feel a teardrop running down her cheek.

"Don't cry, said David brushing away her tear. I will be back on Friday. So every time you think of me, know I am thinking of you."

"On Friday, classes are usually finished by noon. That means I will be on the one-o'clock bus unless I have extra lab work or study in the library. Don't worry; I will be there. I can walk home from the bus station but don't worry, and I will be there."

"Don't forget my lovely one. Auntie has some wedding ideas for you to look at. She said we must decide on a guest list, where the wedding will occur, and our marriage date.

I'm sorry for crying said Hannah sniffing and wiping her eyes with her handkerchief.

"We have the rest of our life to look forward to. We'll start now, Smiled Hannah.

David boarded the bus, placed his belongings on the overhead rack, Sat down, looked out the window, and blew Hannah a kiss. She smiled and returned the kiss.

Hannah and Naomi watched as the bus pulled away.

"Come on, Hannah," said Naomi taking Hannah's arm, let us have a pleasant ride home."

"I have a suggestion for tomorrow," said auntie, guiding Dann-Boys reins. Why don't you, Gwen, Lilly, and Allison come over tomorrow for lunch at about noon and bring Duff and Sam? I have a lot of fabric in my sewing room and the attic. I also have a pattern book to get ideas about the dresses you may want the girls to wear."

"Thank you so much, Naomi; that will be fun, said Hannah. "It is I who should be thankful to you and David. Now I am part of a family."

"That's what all of us want," smiled Hannah.

"Are you sure you want us to bring Sam and Duff?" asked Hannah.

"Yes said Naomi looking at Hannah. Miss Kitty needs some exercise. I thought the boys would chase her around the house. Ring will want to play."

"We can walk to your house tomorrow morning," said Hannah. And be there at about noon. Thank you for a pleasant day. I will dream tonight about David."

"Remember Hannah," said Naomi signaling Danny-Boy to a faster pace. You have school work and the joy of planning your and David's wedding. See you tomorrow."

Lilly greeted Hannah in the front hall. "Was it sad? Did you cry?: asked Lill

"Yes, it was sad, and I did cry, confessed Hannah hugging her sister. But David kept telling me he wasn't very far away."

I" have some fun news for all of us. Tomorrow at about noon, Miss Naomi wants you, Sam, Duff, Allyson, and Gwen to come to her house for lunch. She will show us her fabric collection and talk about colors and style for the bridesmaid's dresses".

Saturday morning, the girls arrived at Miss Naomi's at about twelve-fifteen. Duff rang the buzzer. They could hear Ring barking in the house. Finally, the girls listened to the door unlock. "Welcome, everyone." Said a smiling Miss Naomi. Ring and Miss Kitty ran to the door to find out who was there.

"Auntie, will we have cookies today?" said Sam pulling on Naomi's skirt.

"Yes, there will be cookies, but only at the table or outside," said Naomi leaning down to talk to the little boy.

Ring greeted each guest and then finished his nap by the fireplace. Miss Kitty strutted around the house with her long full tail straight up in the air, curled at the tip like a giant question mark.

"What are we having for lunch?" inquired Duff.

Miss Naomi put her hands on the child's shoulders and said, "We have turkey and vegetable soup with rolls, butter, and jam. You can choose an oatmeal cookie or apple sauce cake for dessert." "After lunch, said Naomi, we will go into my sewing room and look at different fabrics and styles for the bridesmaid's dresses. Then, before we sit down to eat, I have a special surprise for Hanna. After all, the wedding is about the bride."

"I will take you up to the attic where I store most of the bolts of cloth and accessories. David brought all of the fabric to my sewing room. The light is dim in the attic. However, there is one item he didn't bring downstairs," said Naomi.

"Let's go up to the attic, smiled Naomi. We need to take two lamps with us. I am so excited about this."

Hannah felt nervous. She couldn't understand what the surprise was.

Naomi and Hannah ascended the staircase; Naomi pushed the door open at the top landing. Hannah was startled to see a white ghost-like gown on a dress form. Eerie shadows like silhouettes stood at attention on walls and floor.

"Hannah, I want you to have this wedding gown as a gift." "Auntie gasped Hannah. I will take good care of it and give it back to you."

Hannah noticed the dress was decorated with ruffles and accented with pearls, lace, and silk.

I told you it is a gift to keep. You can hand it down to Lilly. Maybe you and David will have a little girl. She will love wearing your wedding dress."

I made this dress for walking down the aisle to marry William. Sadly Will was killed in a train accident a few days before the wedding. If I ever got married, I would make a new dress for that occasion. Right now, the chances of getting married are pretty slim. FOR ME. I don't even have a boyfriend."

I will make alterations so the dress will fit you perfectly. There won't be time today. You can come over after school, and we will work on it. Don't forget the veil. Try it on, said Naomi placing it on Hannah's head.

"You will be a beautiful bride," said Naomi wiping a tear from her eye.

"I feel like a princess. Did you make the veil also?"

"Yes said Naomi proudly. I made the roses by hand, and HAND sewed the appliques on the dress and veil.

"You are so lucky," said Lilly with envy

"Not only will you marry the most handsome man in town, but you also have the most beautiful wedding gown. Oh! I hope I get married and have a nice wedding," swooned Gwen.

"Don't forget, girls, we will look at dresses for you today," reminded Naomi.

"I am so grateful, Miss Naomi; now I will have two dresses!" said Allison

"Auntie, how can I thank you for all of the things you do for us?" said Hannah

"We are family, said Naomi gently. David and I have wanted a family for quite a while, and now we have it."

"Let's go to the dining room and have lunch. Then we can have fun with fabric and patterns," said Naomi.

Sweet was the air with the fragrance of young maidens, waiting for the advent of womanhood with ribbons, bows, satin, and applesauce cake accents.

THOSE LOVELY WEEKENDS

CHAPTER 17

"Lilly, I am so happy today!" exclaimed Hannah. Today is Friday, and I will meet David at the streetcar station.

Naomi will take me this afternoon and bring David and me home. We will spend all weekend together, just him and me!"

"There is one thing that makes me nervous," explained Hannah.

"What is that?" said Lilly brushing Hannah's hair. "Remember the story I told you about Miss Naomi?"

She went to the train station to meet William, the man she would marry. But unfortunately, his train was about seven hours late because there had been a collision between a freight train and a passenger train. And Will was killed. A few days before their wedding. I don't think Naomi has ever gotten over losing her husband-to-be."

Anxiously waiting at the streetcar terminal, Hannah checked the schedule and looked at the big clock on the wall. Soon Hannah saw the streetcar roll into the station ten minutes early. The young couple ran into each other's arms with hugs and kisses. "Thank you, Auntie, for picking us up," said David, brushing a kiss on his auntie's cheek.

"I am glad to do it," said a smiling Naomi. Do you have something special planned for this weekend?"

"Just being together," giggled Hannah. Please let Sister Catherine know I will be home late because David is taking me to dinner,"

"I will drive said, Naomi. That way, you two can make your plans, that is, if David will ride with me again."

"I'm sorry. I know you drive your carriage to work daily and can harness Danny Boy.

"I worry too much about women folk driving the carriage. I know they can do it, but most women are so small," and the horses are so big, they could run away if they got spooked"

"David, you better get used to women driving carriages and other things. A day will come when we can vote, be a doctor," or do anything else we may want to do."

"I agree with you, Naomi; women can do more than raise children and cook all day," said Hannah.

"I know I am outnumbered in this conversation." laughed David, opening the carriage door for Hannah. He slipped into the seat and gathered Hannah in his arms with a passionate kiss. 'Do you have any suggestions as to what you want to do tonight," asked David

"Yes, said Hannah, I want to spend as much time with you as possible."

"Would you like to go to the Atlantic Side Hotel for dinner and dancing? That way, we can be together longer," suggests David. "I will have to go home, change my dress and comb my hair before I can go to dinner." Replied Hannah.

"You look beautiful," said David. Friday night is informal. I think the dancing starts at about eight o'clock."

"That is a wonderful idea, said Hannah. I didn't have lunch, so that we can go to dinner anytime."

"I have another idea, said David smiling at Hannah. We can go dancing tomorrow night at the Atlantic Side Hotel. It is formal, you can wear your prettiest ball gown, and I will wear my tuxedo. I think the Saturday night dances have the best music. We will stay out as late as we can." Saturday I can take you shopping and out to lunch. I also need to spend some time with Duff and Sam.

Sunday morning, I thought we could go to Mass at St Luke's Cathedral near the hotel."

"Maybe we can make an appointment to talk to a secretary that takes care of weddings. Whatever you decide, Hannah is fine with me. I think Naomi would like to have the wedding at St Luke's. She has a lot of friends to invite."

'All of that is okay with me, said Hannah. I want to walk down that aisle and marry you. It doesn't matter what church we are married in; I want to be your wife."

David and Hannah spent lovely days and evenings together with accents of love and roses.

THE WEDDING OF DAVID AND HANNAH

CHAPTER 18

Leo danced her way into August, leaving colors of lovely periods in exquisite shades of deepest gold and yellow. The date was August fourteenth. Hannah and David are sitting outside on the porch swing of their future home. On August sixteenth, the couple will be married at two pm at St Luke's Cathedral, a few blocks from the Atlantic Side Hotel, where they will enjoy their reception.

"I think we are about ready for our wedding," said David putting his arm around Hannah.

"Yes, said Hannah, examining the wrinkled sheet of paper she took out of her apron pocket. I will read you what we have done, and you tell me if we have forgotten anything," said Hannah smiling at David.

"Fred will pick up grandfather the day of the rehearsal dinner. He will stay two nights at Auntie's house. He is so happy to be a part of the wedding. Our family is growing.

"I have checked off the following items. Said Hannah. You, Fred, and Naomi will bring everything to the church on Friday. The bakery and florist will deliver the cake and flowers to the hotel. All of us will get ready there on Saturday morning. I think some of my aunties friends will help with hair and makeup. The girls love their colorful dresses and flowers. Sam and Duff will be adorable in their little suits. I love the beautiful gown and veil Naomi has made for me. She hasn't said what she is going to wear. She said she couldn't decide. We have lunch planned at the Hotel for the reception; unsure of the menu, laughed Hannah. The flowers and cake have been ordered. The church organist will play the music, and the singer will sing our favorite songs. We have reservations about staying at the Atlantic the first night. Naomi will host the rehearsal dinner at the church the night before the wedding at six o'clock. We sign the final papers for the adoption of Duff and Sam. after the wedding. We have to be married to complete the adoption paperwork." I am so excited that the boys will legally be our sons."

"I have a surprise for you, Hannah, said David taking an envelope from his pocket. Remember when we made reservations in Atlantic City for our honeymoon? This letter is from the hotel "The Atlantic Club, in Atlantic City " confirming our ten-day reservations. The reservation says we are on the beach; I can hardly wait to walk the beach and boardwalk."

"David, how far is it to Atlantic City from New York City?" "I think it is a little over a hundred miles," said David looking at the brochure. Auntie will take us to the streetcar station. Then we have a short ride to the train station. It will be a busy day."

"I will miss Sam and Duff, sighed Hannah. I hope Naomi, Lilly, Gwen, and Allison will take good care of them".

"Don't worry, " laughed David " Four ladies should be able to take care of two little boys."

"Maybe we should take them with us, teased Hannah. We could get a room with two double beds. Or all of us could sleep in one bed."

"Yes, that would be fun, said David. Sam would get up during the night. I will suddenly feel a tap on my shoulder. I know it is not you. It will be Sam. He will say, "what are you doing, papa?"

"So said Hannah, what are you doing, papa?" She hid her blushing face in her hands.

"When I can take a few days off, we can have a camping and fishing vacation," promised David. I think the kids would enjoy sleeping in a tent and fishing. It is fun to plan a family vacation and a holiday for the two of us."

"I agree with you," said Hannah kissing David on his forehead. However, you will have to keep me safe from critters of the night and bugs."

"You would do that?" said David, sleep in a tent and cook over a campfire?"

"I don't chop wood or clean fish. I will cook the fish."

"I can imagine what Sam would look like if he cleaned a fish, and you know you will teach him how to do it, said Hannah. But, I am not sure if Duff would do it; he likes to stay clean."

"I have never slept in a tent Said Hannah; I think it would be fun.

"We can sing songs around the campfire after supper," said David.

"I am trying to imagine what it will be like locked up in a tent with Sam. Giggled Hannah. You know how Duff complains about Sam."

"I know said David smiling. Duff says Sam smells bad, wears dirty socks to bed, and doesn't always wash his hands before eating. Sometimes Ring gets up and leaves the bedroom."

"I love Sam just the way he is. I don't want him to change," said Hannah.

"I feel the same way about Duff. He is organized and likes to keep himself and things neat and in order," said David.

"I do worry about Duff's health. He doesn't have much energy for a little boy and has dark circles under his eyes. I am going to make an appointment for him at the City Hospital. He is very loveable. Said David with compassion. The boys are a blessing to our family."

"I love that Duff and Sam will be junior groomsmen in our wedding. We want them to feel like the four of us are family," said Hannah.

"We have a ten o'clock meeting tomorrow with the electrical and plumbing contractors. They said it would be more efficient to lay all the pipes and the electrical wiring before the painter and wallpaper arrive. Sometimes walls and floors must be torn up, so we should do things in order," said David.

"What rooms will start with lights?" asked Hannah.

We will have a light in the kitchen, service porch, dining room, bedrooms, and downstairs bathroom under the stairs." Said s David.

"We are going to live in luxury," said Hannah. All we have to do is turn on a light. The best part is we will have a bathroom in the house. I hate going outside in the cold and dark. You are spoiling us."

"It's my pleasure." Said, David. I want to take good care of my family."

"I also ordered a hot water tank, explained David. I am assuming the plumber will connect it to the kitchen stove. So we should have hot water most of the time."

"Hannah, it is getting late. It is almost six-thirty. I would love to take you to dinner," said David. Where would you like to go

"Jordan Sandwich Shop is fine. I like their chicken dinners; soon, you will have to get used to my chicken dinners," replied Hanna

"I will see you at rehearsal dinner. The next day will be our wedding, and I can hardly wait." Said, David.

Hannah tiptoed into her bedroom. Lilly was reading, and the boys were not in bed.

"Where are the children?" asked Hannah in a low voice. "Gwen wanted Sam to spend the night with the Duff. All of

us know you are very busy." Replied Lilly.

"You are right about that, yawned Hannah. I am so tired. Miss Naomi has a busy schedule for all of us. I will let you read her plan, and we better be on time. I am glad she knows what to do; she always plans a beautiful wedding."

"David and I talked for hours about the house. While we are on our honeymoon in Atlantic City, the plumbing contractor and the electrician will be there. They may have to tear up some of the walls or floors. The Painting and wallpaper contractors will come in last. There will be a lot more things that we have to do.

"Don't worry about it, said, Lilly. I will help make curtains and wash windows. You will get it all done."

"I know, said Hannah, yawning again. Everything seems so overwhelming. I will also have to look after the boys and David and cook and wash clothes."

I wish I had those problems, said Lilly. But, unfortunately, I don't even have a boyfriend."

"I don't mean to complain said Hannah; I want to be a good wife and mother. Maybe David and I will have our child, and maybe it will be a girl! We know we love little boys. We will love" a little girl the same."

"We better get to sleep. Tomorrow will be hectic. Naomi wants all of us to be in our wedding clothes at the church by eleven o'clock. She wants to check the hems on dresses and ensure everything is perfect. ."I don't know what David and I would do suppose we didn't have her advice and help. I hope she will get married someday."

"Goodnight, Lilly"

"Goodnight, Mrs. Kilmore," replied Lilly."

Hannah woke early on August sixteenth. The sun was shining bright like rays from the Good Shepherd's Crown.

"Lilly, did you enjoy the rehearsal dinner last night? Do you know what you are to do? Today is the real thing."

"Yes said, Lilly. I love to get dressed up for a party. Miss Naomi said we could keep the dresses for the next occasion or event."

"I just thought of something else, said Hannah. I won't be sleeping in this room or living in this home anymore. I-I will be with David. Hannah felt her face blushing. I don't know for sure what David wants from me."

"Don't worry said, Lilly. David may be nervous too. Didn't the two of you talk to Sister Catherine"?

"Yes, we did. Sister Catherine said the marriage bed is part of our love for each other.

We also talked with and prayed with Father Andrew. He will officiate at the wedding."

"Another thing that has me worried said, Hannah. I don't want to do something stupid like a trip or say something wrong. This wedding dress is heavy."

"Don't' worry, said Lilly; David will have his eye on you, and I am your bridesmaid of honor."

"Well said Naomi to David while pouring him some coffee, you will no longer be single by the end of the day. Are you ready for this life change?" Yes, said David sipping his coffee. "I "Have waited for this day all of my life. Said, David. I am excited and nervous. Grandfather has taught me the facts of life and things I should know. I think he loved grandmother the way I love Hannah. She is shy. That is one of the things that attracted me to her. I love it when she blushes. Love is hard to explain. Sometimes I see grandfather sleeping, and he smiles; I know his dreams are of grandma. Sometimes he sheds tears if we talk about grandmother. Grandfather says she is all around him. Another thing he taught me is there is nothing more enduring than a woman's touch."

The bridal party arrived at St Mark's Cathedral in a white carriage drawn by two white horses driven by best man Fred.

They hurried to a dressing room at the side of the narthex.

"I am nervous said Allison; I have never seen so many people. Don't worry said Gwen; Lilly and I are here with you."

Miss Naomi stepped into the room to check everyone's dresses and hair. She adjusted bows and fluffed ruffles. "You girls, wait here, and I will tell you when it is time to go down the aisle." The groomsmen arrived at the church in a black carriage driven by David and pulled by Danny Boy 'Earl, and Sam and Duff completed the party. They hurried to their dressing room and were greeted by Naomi.

"I want to be sure all of you are ready and check your bowties. I will signal you when it is time to enter the sanctuary from the room on the side.

The church of olden times stood tall with its arched stained glass windows supported by heavy oak beams. The stained glass windows tell the story of God and His love. The wedding party waited for the signal from the organist to begin the processional to the exquisite music of Wagner's The Wedding March."

The aisle is decorated with plump white baskets full of deep fragrant lavender to palest pink roses and carnations accented with sprays of baby's breath, ivy, and ribbon.

The wedding party slowly walked down the aisle. Allison was beautiful and petite in a rose and pink plaid taffeta dress. She had a solid pink sash around her waist and carried a single pink rose, and a pink ribbon was in her hair.

Gwen's dress is a lovely shade of lavender floral with a pink sash around her waist. She carried a single red rose and had a red ribbon in her hair.

Lilly, the maid of honor, was elegant and confident in a solid rose pink taffeta dress with a floral pink sash around her waist. She carried a single pink rose and had a pink ribbon in her hair.

David and the groomsmen Fred, Earl, and Sam, Duffentered the sanctuary from a side entrance.

"Are you nervous, Hannah?" whispered Eric.

"Yes, replied Hannah. Soon I will be Mrs. David Kilmore." "I am proud of you, and you are beautiful; I am honored that you asked me to walk you down the aisle," said Eric.

Naomi and her father stand in place of the bride and grooms parents. Georgie Gruen carried a sating pillow holding the wedding rings, and he escorted his little sister, flower girl Ivy Lea. "David is so handsome, thought Hannah; I will soon be his wife. I love him so much. I will never walk away; I will go to him." Mary Beth Jordan thought David was handsome, and she was sure he would notice her before he saw Hannah. But deep down in her broken heart, she knew David wasn't looking for her; he was waiting for Hannah. He always looked at Hannah. David and I have known each other most of our lives, and she was heartbroken that she was not the one in the white dress. Doesn't David knows by now that I love him?"

HANNAH

Betsy almost felt faint at the thought that she would never be David's wife.

As Hannah came down the aisle, she could not take her eyes off David. He never quit smiling and quickly brushed a tear from his eye.

When the bride got to the alter, Sister Lois, in her soprano voice, sang Schubert's Ava Marie.

The priest greeted the assembly with an opening prayer, liturgy, the first reading of the scripture of the Old Testament, and a lesson from the Gospels and homily.

" David and Hannah are invited to declare their intention of marriage and exchange rings."

Holding hands and gazing into eyes each other, the bride and groom promise to be faithful to each other, and only at death will they part. David took Hannah into his arms and kissed her.
Irish Tenor Father Andrew sang the Lord's Prayer accompanied by the church choir.

The priest blesses the couple.

"I would like to introduce the new Dr. David and Mrs. Hannah Rose Kilmore. They have asked me to make a few announcements. A receiving line and reception will be at the Atlantic Side Hotel, about two blocks from here. All of you are invited. Dr. and Mrs. Kilmore also have an extraordinary announcement."

The "Two little lads, Samuel Eli David, age six, and Duff Eric Gregory, age eight, will officially be the adopted sons of Hannah and David. The adoption becomes official at the signing of papers today. We ask God's blessing on this young family."

The guests responded .with applause and congratulations.

Hannah and David signed the papers, and the new family has whisked away to the hotel in their white carriage.

"That was a beautiful ceremony, said granny to Betsy. Are you sure you want to go to the reception?"

"Yes, sniffed Mary Beth; I couldn't feel worse. My heart is fragile; I don't think I will ever get over David. Every time I see him, I want to kiss him. Why is love so sad and so "beautiful?"

The bride and groom arrived at the Atlantic Side Hotel for their reception. The guest greeted the nuptials with more congratulations—baskets brimming with flowers from the ceremony decorated the room. The bridesmaids added their flower bouquets to the buffet table, giving an elegant look to silver platters of plump sandwiches and various salads heaped into crystal bowls and condiments. Crowded trays of savory chicken, roast beef, and spicy ham are served. The cake table is decorated with David's great-grandmother Kilmore's Irish linen tablecloth. Complete with silver knife and spatula. Hannah chose a traditional American white wedding cake with buttercream icing and custard filling between the three-tier cake layers. Coffee, tea, and punch accompanied the cake.

Naomi lined up everyone for the receiving line. There was a lot of hugging, shaking hands, and kisses.

"Betsy do you want to go thru the receiving line or go home?" inquired Granny Jorden.

"I am going thru the line. I can't touch David or get close to him. Mary Beth is the last time I talked to him, and I love his cologne. His hair is always perfectly combed, and he has a funny little curl that falls on his forehead," said Mary Beth lightly. He dresses perfectly, and his jeans are tight-fitting. Granny, this is so hard. I will think about them sleeping together. Why can't that be me?" "Betsy, why don't you ask grandpa to take you home?" suggested Granny.

"Another thing, granny, Hannah isn't even jealous of me. She doesn't care; she is the one that has him."

"Betsy, let's go thru the reception; line, then get something to eat. The food table is beautiful."

"I will greet Hannah and David and be gracious, " said Mary Beth.

"Congratulations, David and Hannah. I hope you are happy," said Mary Beth.

"We are always happy," said David winking at Hann."We are always happy," said David winking at Hannah.

"Come on, David, we have to dance our first dance as a married couple." Said Hannah leading him to the dance floor.

The guests applauded while David gathered Hannah in his arms and tenderly kissed her.

"It is almost eight o'clock said Naomi to David and Hannah. Most of the guests have left. Your luggage is in your room. Leave your wedding clothes there, and the girls and I will pick them up tomorrow. Loretta will help me pack the gifts and flowers and take them to my house. Remember, you can use a back stairway to get to your room. So leave, and hopefully, no one will see you.

Have a good time in Atlantic City, don't worry about the boys. We will take good care of them."

Hannah and David looked around the room and hurried up the back stairway. David searches his pockets for the keys.

"Hannah, I can't find the keys."

"I have them said Hannah, jiggling the keys and laughing.

You dropped them and didn't know it."

David unlocked the door and motioned Hannah to walk in first. Then, he softly closed the door and looked at his lovely bride with hungry eyes.

www.ingramcontent.com/pod-product-compliance
Lightning Source LLC
LaVergne TN
LVHW011942070526
838202LV00054B/4754